JESS THE BORDER COLLIE
The Challenge

Jess darted forward and gently rolled the bottle back towards the tiny lamb. The animal fastened on to it again, closing his eyes with pleasure as he sucked on the teat.

'Good boy, Jess!' Jenny congratulated him.

'Look at that!' said Ian. 'Now there are three of us feeding the lambs. It's a pity Jess can't help out like that in the fields. Matt was telling me that some of the lambs aren't getting enough nourishment and they might die.'

Jenny nodded. 'Even lambs in the fields sometimes need extra feeding,' she replied. 'But, without more help, we just can't get round them all.'

She watched Jess. 'Ian,' she said. 'I've just had the most marvellous idea . . .'

Also by Lucy Daniels

TV Tie-in titles
Jess the Border Collie 1: The Arrival
Jess the Border Collie 2: The Challenge
Jess the Border Collie 3: The Runaway

Animal Ark Classics

Kittens in the Kitchen
Pony in the Porch
Dolphin in the Deep
Bunnies in the Bathroom
Puppies in the Pantry
Hamster in a Hamper
Horse in the House
Badger in the Basement
Cub in the Cupboard
Guinea-Pig in the Garage
Puppy in a Puddle
Hedgehogs in the Hall
Lamb in the Laundry
Foals in the Field
Koalas in a Crisis

With a special foreword from Lucy Daniels

For a full list of available Animal Ark titles,
see www.madaboutbooks.com

Jess
The Border Collie

the Challenge

LUCY DANIELS

Hodder
Children's
Books

a division of Hodder Headline Limited

Special thanks to Helen Magee

Text copyright © 1998 Ben M. Baglio
Created by Ben M. Baglio, London W12 7QY
Illustrations copyright © 1998 Trevor Parkin

First published in Great Britain in 1998
by Hodder Children's Books
This edition published in 2005

1

A Catalogue record for this book is available
from the British Library

ISBN   0 340 91709 1

Typeset in Bembo by Avon DataSet Ltd,
Bidford on Avon, Warwickshire

Printed and bound in Great Britain by
Bookmarque Ltd, Croydon, Surrey

The paper and board used in this paperback by Hodder Children's Books
are natural recyclable products made from wood grown in sustainable
forests. The manufacturing processes conform to the environmental
regulations of the country of origin.

Hodder Children's Books
a division of Hodder Headline Ltd
338 Euston Road
London NW1 3BH

1

'Fetch, Jess!' Jenny Miles called, throwing a stick into the sea. She shaded her eyes with her hand. The early spring sunshine glittered on the waves as they curled towards the shore. Jess, Jenny's sheepdog puppy, scampered into the sparkling water and swam strongly towards the floating stick.

'His leg's really much better now, isn't it?' commented Carrie, Jenny's best friend.

Jenny nodded happily as Jess retrieved the stick and swam towards her. Jess had been born with a badly twisted leg. At first, Jenny's father had wanted to put the little puppy down but Jenny had persuaded him to let her look after the runt of the litter – and now Jess was a happy, healthy puppy, even though his leg had had to be in a cast for a while.

'He only limps a little now,' Jenny replied. 'Nobody notices – well, almost nobody.'

Carrie looked sympathetically at her friend. 'Nobody except Fiona McLay, you mean,' she said. 'Don't take any notice of what she says. She's only jealous.'

Fiona McLay was in Jenny's class at Graston School. She was always taunting Jenny about not having the right kind of trainers or wearing fashionable clothes. Jenny didn't care about clothes, but Fiona's spitefulness still hurt.

Fiona had started calling Jess 'Jenny's lame dog'.

'*Jealous*?' echoed Jenny, turning to Carrie in surprise. The wind whipped her shoulder-length honey-brown hair into her eyes and she shoved it back from her face. 'Why on earth would Fiona McLay be jealous of *me*? Her parents are really well off. She has everything she wants.'

'Because you've got the best dog in the world and he's *famous*, after his picture was used for the animal welfare campaign,' Carrie replied.

Carrie's mum was an artist. They lived in Cliffbay, a fishing village not far from Windy Hill, the farm where Jenny lived. Mrs Turner had painted Jess for an advertising campaign to help maltreated animals. Jenny still couldn't get used to seeing Jess's picture on posters and in newspapers. He looked so small and vulnerable with his leg still in its cast. She bent down as Jess came hurtling out of the water towards her, sending up glittering sprays of seawater. He was a lot bigger now.

'Ow!' she yelled as Jess dropped the stick on her feet and then shook himself. 'I'm so wet now, I might as well have gone for the stick myself!'

Jess looked up at her and wagged his tail. Jenny laughed. 'Home now,' she said firmly. 'Mrs Grace will have tea ready.'

'You like Mrs Grace, don't you?' Carrie

asked, as they walked along the beach.

Jenny nodded. 'At first I didn't want a housekeeper at Windy Hill,' she explained. 'I thought we could manage all right the way we were but I'm really glad we've got Mrs Grace now.'

'What about Ian?' Carrie went on.

Jenny pulled a face. Ian Amery was Mrs Grace's nephew. He was staying with his aunt until his parents got themselves settled in Canada, and it looked like being quite a long visit.

'We didn't get off to a very good start,' Jenny said, remembering how she had accused Ian of letting her father's sheep out of the cliff field. 'He still hasn't forgiven me for calling him an idiot.'

Carrie giggled and tossed her bright red hair out of her eyes. She had a dusting of freckles over her nose and bright blue eyes. 'I can't imagine you getting angry,' she said. 'You're usually so calm.'

Jenny blushed. 'It was the sheep,' she said. 'I thought he had put them in danger.'

'And sheep are important,' Carrie stated.

'Of course,' replied Jenny. 'This is Border country. Sheep are *everything*.'

'Especially at lambing time,' Carrie agreed. 'How is your dad getting on?'

Jenny frowned. 'Poor Dad,' she sighed. 'He's exhausted. There's so much work to do, and Calum McLay has offered higher wages to the casual workers Dad usually employs for the lambing. Dad just can't afford to compete with that, so the workers have gone to the McLays' farm instead of Windy Hill. Dad is going to be really overworked this lambing.'

'Can't Matt help?' asked Carrie.

'Matt only comes home from college at weekends,' Jenny explained. 'Dad won't let him interrupt his studies to help on the farm.'

Matt was Jenny's eighteen-year-old brother. He was away at agricultural college.

'Your dad won't have to sell Windy Hill, will he?' asked Carrie, concerned.

Jenny sighed. 'I hope not,' she said fervently. 'If the lambing is good then things should be all right. Dad doesn't talk about it much but I know it's touch and go.' She lifted her head to look far down the beach to where the cliffs rose to the fields above – and Windy Hill. 'I think I'd *die* if I had to leave Windy Hill,' she said.

Carrie whirled round and put a hand on each of Jenny's shoulders. 'You won't have to,' she said firmly, her blue eyes unusually serious. 'You're Jenny of Windy Hill. It's where you belong.'

Jenny gave a shaky smile and her chin came up. 'Of course I won't,' she said.

'And don't let Fiona McLay get you down either,' Carrie continued. 'Remember what I said. She's just jealous!'

'Oh, Carrie,' Jenny laughed. 'You always make me feel better!'

Carrie grinned. 'Mum says there's an up side to everything,' she declared. 'It just takes a bit of finding sometimes – that's all.'

'I'll remember that,' said Jenny, whistling to Jess as they reached the path to Cliffbay. 'See you at school tomorrow.'

Jenny made her way up the winding track that led from the beach to the clifftop. At the top she stood for a moment, shading her eyes against the sun. The wind teased at her hair and ruffled Jess's black and white coat. The sea gleamed silver in the spring sunshine and Puffin Island lay like a green jewel in its silver setting. Carrie's dad ran trips to Puffin Island in his boat. The island was a bird sanctuary. Jenny had never been there but she hoped to go some time soon.

She turned and looked inland. From here she could see the ruins of Darktarn Keep standing high on its hill. The keep was Jenny's favourite place – especially when she was upset. She let her eyes move down to the farm fields stretching below the keep to the clifftop. They were dotted with sheep.

Fraser Miles, Jenny's father, bred Scottish Blackfaces, which were a hardy hill breed. The climate could often be harsh here on the border of England and Scotland – even in the spring at lambing time. Border sheep needed to be tough enough to withstand everything the weather could throw at them.

Jenny was looking forward to the lambing, despite the problems. She loved the tiny newborn lambs with their sweet little black faces. Last year at this time her mother had still been here to help with the lambing. But that was last year and now her mother was dead, killed in a riding accident shortly after last year's lambing had finished. The lambing was going to bring back memories for all of them, especially her father.

Jenny brushed a tear away as she shifted her gaze to the farm buildings in the distance, remembering how things used to be. The farmhouse stood four-square in the middle of the fields, its red-tiled roof gleaming in the sunlight. Windy Hill – her home. She raised her head and let the wind blow through her hair.

'Carrie's right,' she said to Jess. 'I'm Jenny of Windy Hill – and you're Jess of Windy Hill. Come on, let's go home.'

'Just in time. Tea's ready,' said Mrs Grace comfortably, as Jenny came into the big farmhouse kitchen with Jess at her heels. The little dog scampered up to Ellen Grace and rubbed himself against her legs.

'Don't worry, you'll get fed too,' said Mrs Grace to him, patting his head affectionately.

Jenny smiled. Mrs Grace and Jess got along really well.

'Is Dad in from the fields yet?' she asked, going to the dresser that ran along one wall of the kitchen and taking down a stack of blue-patterned plates.

'He's just gone up to check on the fences in the top field,' Mrs Grace replied. 'He should be back soon.'

Jenny frowned. 'Those fences belong to Calum McLay,' she said, setting out the plates.

Mrs Grace nodded. 'Your father is worried about them. They're in need of some repair and you know what ewes are like when it comes to lambing time. They've got a tendency to bolt.'

Jenny knew that ewes in labour sometimes took fright and ran off. 'If they got out of the field they'd be on McLay land,' she said.

'And then there would be trouble,' agreed Mrs Grace.

Jenny frowned. Calum McLay was Fiona's father. He wanted to acquire more land to plant trees – trees in sheep country! Jenny thought it was outrageous. But that wasn't the worst of the problem. Calum McLay was determined to take over Windy Hill – by hook or by crook.

'Now, now, don't you go worrying over the lambing,' Mrs Grace advised Jenny. 'Lambing might be a hard time on a farm like this but there's the common riding at the end of it to look forward to.' The common riding was when all the towns and villages in the Borders turned out to ride round the boundaries or marches of their towns.

Jenny smiled suddenly and her whole face lit up. Mrs Grace looked at her heart-shaped face framed by her honey-coloured hair. 'You know, you look just like your mother, when you smile like that,' she said.

'I was thinking about her up on the cliffs,' Jenny replied. 'I was trying to remember all the good times we had – like the stories she used to tell me about the Border reivers. I'm glad I look like her.'

'You're a lot quieter than your mum was, though,' Mrs Grace went on. 'I remember her as a girl. She was always a bit of a daredevil but she enjoyed life. She could always make me laugh.'

Jenny's cheeks flushed pink with pleasure at the memory of how her mother had been able to make *all* of them laugh. It was good to talk to Mrs Grace about her mother. Jenny's father never talked about her. He still found the whole subject too painful.

'I like talking to you about Mum, Mrs Grace,' Jenny confided. 'The more I talk about her, the more I remember.' She hesitated a moment, looking down at Jess. The puppy licked her hand, sensing her sudden sadness. 'Sometimes I'm afraid I'll forget her,' Jenny finished.

Ellen Grace put her arm round Jenny's shoulders. 'You'll never do that,' she comforted her. 'All you have to do is look in a mirror. I think it's your hair. It's the exact shade your mum's was.'

'I'd really like to get it cut,' Jenny said. 'It's a pest. It blows into my eyes all the time.'

'Where's that hair-tie I got for you?' Mrs Grace asked.

Jenny dug in her jeans pocket and pulled out a blue and yellow hair-tie. She twisted her hair into a knot and fastened it with the tie.

'One day I'm going to fix your hair properly,' said Mrs Grace.

Jenny pulled a face and Ellen Grace laughed. 'We'll get it properly done for the common riding,' she said. 'Everybody gets dressed up for that.'

The Graston common riding was in May and Jenny was really looking forward to it. It was the biggest day of the year. The lambing would be over, all the really hard work done, and there would be time to celebrate – if the lambing went well.

'Are you on the common riding committee?' she asked Mrs Grace.

Ellen Grace bent down to open the oven door of the Aga and took out a big shepherd's pie. The potato topping was browned to a turn and it smelled delicious. 'I certainly am,' she said, laying the pie dish on top of the Aga to keep warm. 'And I hope I'll get some help from you. I've got a mound of baking to do as well as making bunting and helping to decorate the floats for the procession.'

Jenny looked into Ellen Grace's warm blue eyes. 'I'd love to help,' she said, smiling.

THE CHALLENGE

The kitchen door opened just then, and Fraser Miles entered. 'Something smells good,' he said.

Ellen Grace put her hands on her hips and tried to look severe. 'And about time too,' she said. 'That pie is nearly ruined.'

Fraser Miles just laughed. 'That'll be the day, when anything you cook is ruined, Ellen,' he said, as he passed Jenny and ruffled her hair. 'How's my lass?'

Jenny looked up at him and saw the weariness and worry behind his smile. 'Fine,' she said. 'What about the fences?'

Her father ran a hand through his hair and shook his head. 'They need attention, that's for sure,' he said. 'I've contacted McLay about it, but the fences were just as bad when I went up there just now.'

'Can't *you* fix them?' asked Jenny, concerned. 'If our sheep get out we could lose them.'

'I don't think Calum would take too kindly to my interfering with his fences,' Mr Miles answered her. 'But it might come to that.'

Jenny studied her father more closely. He looked exhausted. Jess lolloped up and wagged

13

his tail. Fraser Miles gave the puppy a brief pat. Jess scampered off to the corner of the kitchen and picked up a slipper in his mouth. He trotted back and laid the slipper in front of Mr Miles.

Fraser laughed. 'If you go on like this I might be glad we kept you after all,' he said.

Jess barked and Jenny felt a warm glow. Her father had been dead against keeping Jess. His own dogs, Jake and Nell, were working sheepdogs and never came into the house. Fraser Miles always said animals had to earn their keep on a farm. But Jenny had great hopes that he would love Jess as much as she did – in time.

There was a sound from the farmyard and Mrs Grace looked out of the window. 'Uh-oh!' she said. 'It's Calum McLay.'

Fraser turned at once. 'What on earth does *he* want?' he said in exasperation. 'As if he isn't causing me enough problems with his fencing!'

Jenny watched her father stride out of the kitchen into the farmyard and went to stand by the open window with Mrs Grace.

A big, burly man was getting out of a Land Rover. He slammed the door and stomped

THE CHALLENGE

across the yard to meet Fraser. Hands on hips, Mr McLay stopped and stood with his feet planted firmly on the cobbles of the yard.

'He acts as if he owns the place,' Jenny muttered.

'What can I do for you, Calum?' Fraser Miles said politely.

Calum McLay thrust his chin forward, his heavy face red with anger. 'You can stay off my land, that's what you can do,' he said.

Fraser Miles looked down for a moment. Jenny could see him holding on to his temper. Then he looked up and said, his voice calm, 'I haven't been on your land, Calum.'

'You've been messing around with my fences!' the other man yelled, taking a step forward.

'Your fences need fixing,' Fraser replied quietly.

Jenny saw that Calum McLay's face was getting redder by the minute. Even his short black hair seemed to bristle with anger. It was as if Mr Miles's calmness made him all the madder.

The big man stuck out a finger, stabbing the

air in front of Fraser Miles's face. 'If you mess around with my fences, I'll have you up for trespass!'

'Your fences are putting my sheep at risk,' Fraser said reasonably.

Calum McLay drew himself up. '*Your* sheep are *your* business,' he sneered. 'And a poor sort of business you're making of them as far as I can make out. You can't afford the wages I'm paying so you can't get help. You can't handle the lambing on your own and you know it. You're finished, Miles. Why don't you give in and sell out now – to me?'

Fraser Miles looked down again. He was being very patient with Calum McLay. Jenny held her breath as the silence went on.

Even Calum McLay grew uncomfortable, shifting from foot to foot. 'Well?' he said at last, his voice cracking slightly.

'You won't get Windy Hill, Calum,' Mr Miles replied very quietly – so quietly that Jenny could hardly hear him through the open window. 'Not while I'm alive.'

Calum McLay swallowed hard and looked away. 'Just keep off my land,' he blustered, making for his Land Rover. 'You touch my fences and I'll prosecute – I mean it. Then where will your precious Windy Hill be?' Then he got into the Land Rover and drove off, racing the engine.

Fraser Miles stood quite still in the middle of the farmyard, his head down. Jenny felt a touch on her arm.

'Come on, love,' Mrs Grace said. 'Let's just pop this pie back in the oven for a moment. Your father will be wanting a bit of time to himself.'

Jenny watched as her father moved slowly towards the farm gate and stood looking out over the land belonging to his beloved Windy Hill.

'OK,' she said, her throat tight. 'It won't matter if it's a bit burnt, will it?'

'It won't matter at all,' said Mrs Grace. 'And don't you worry about Windy Hill. Your father will keep it safe.'

Jenny nodded, trying to hold back tears. Her father wasn't a magician. He couldn't do the impossible. She was old enough to know how hard things were for him. If he went bankrupt the farm would be sold to the highest bidder — and that was sure to be Calum McLay. Why was Calum McLay so intent on ruining her father? Why did he want Windy Hill so much? She stole a brief look out of the window at Fraser Miles's uncompromising back. One thing was sure. She couldn't ask her father.

2

Jenny was riding her bike down the farm track on her way to school the next day when she noticed her father in the bottom field. He was standing quite still, looking at a ewe. Jake and Nell lay beside him, also perfectly still. Jenny braked and drew into the side of the track. At that moment her father turned and saw her. He beckoned to her and Jenny dismounted, scrambling over the drystone wall that separated the field from the track. Her father held his finger to his lips and, as he did so, Jenny looked beyond him.

The ewe was pawing the ground and bleating softly. The breath caught in Jenny's throat. She had seen enough pregnant ewes to know the signs. This one was about to give birth.

'The first Windy Hill lamb of the season,' her father whispered softly to Jenny as she reached him. 'It shouldn't be long now.'

Almost as he spoke, the ewe lay down with her legs stretched out to one side and began to strain. Jenny and her father were about twenty metres away but Jenny knew Fraser wouldn't go any closer, not unless the ewe looked as if she were in trouble. Ewes frequently gave up the attempt to lamb if they had an audience.

'Is she coping all right?' asked Jenny.

Fraser nodded. 'I don't often get to see the very first lamb,' he said. 'Usually I come out one morning and find that a dozen or more have been born during the night. I just couldn't resist watching this one.'

Jenny looked at her father, standing quietly beside her. There was real excitement on his face.

Even after all these years of lambing, the thought of the first lamb still meant so much to him.

'Look, Jenny!' he said softly. 'Here it comes.'

Jenny shifted her gaze to the ewe. As she watched, the animal began to strain harder, raising her head and curling her top lip. The waterbag, a transparent membrane enclosing the lamb, began to appear. It slid gently from the ewe's body and on to the ground behind the mother. As it did so, the waterbag burst, and Jenny gasped as the lamb's nose and front feet appeared. She heard her father sigh.

'That's OK,' he said. 'If the waterbag hadn't burst we'd have needed to do something about it, otherwise the lamb could suffocate.'

Jenny was barely listening. She was gazing in wonder as the tiny lamb began to kick and cough. The ewe turned and started to lick her baby.

'Oh, Dad, isn't it wonderful?' she breathed.

Her father looked at her, smiling. 'It's the best sight in the world,' he said. 'A good birth and a healthy lamb. That licking will dry the little fellow and establish a bond between lamb and ewe,' her father told her.

Jenny knew that sometimes a ewe failed to bond with her lamb and then a substitute mother had to be found. But these two looked as if they were going to be all right. The ewe was nuzzling her baby, licking furiously to stimulate its circulation. Early lambs often died of hypothermia.

Jenny shivered in the chill breeze off the sea. 'Will the lamb be warm enough?' she asked her father.

Fraser Miles looked out to sea. The wind was whipping spray off the tops of the waves. 'I'd rather get them both to a more sheltered spot,' he confessed. 'It's a bit exposed just here. Have you got time to give me a hand, lass?'

Jenny looked at her watch. 'Just about,' she replied, delighted. 'What do you want me to do?'

Her father pointed towards the drystone wall. 'If we can get them under the lee of the wall, that'll keep the wind off them,' he said. 'But we have to make sure the ewe doesn't lose contact with the lamb. If she loses sight of it she'll return to the spot she chose for the birth and abandon the lamb.'

'So how do we manage that?' asked Jenny.

'If you can take the lamb by the front legs and draw it along the ground in the direction we want the ewe to go then the ewe will follow,' Fraser Miles told her.

'But won't that hurt the lamb?' Jenny asked.

Mr Miles shook his head. 'Not if you're careful. The lamb must stay on the ground so that the ewe can continue to lick it as we move.'

Jenny and her father moved quietly towards the ewe. 'Just take the legs,' Fraser instructed as Jenny hesitated. 'I'll clear the afterbirth away.'

Jenny did as she was told, grasping the little animal's front legs firmly but gently between her hands. Then she began to draw the lamb along the grass towards the spot her father had chosen. The ewe followed, head down, licking her lamb.

'That's it, Jenny. You're doing fine,' her father encouraged her.

Jenny laid the tiny lamb down in the shelter of the wall and watched as the ewe settled down to take care of her baby.

'Just one more job to do,' Fraser Miles said.

Jenny watched as her father drew his thumb

and forefinger gently down the ewe's teats.

'That breaks the seal at the end,' he said. 'Now the lamb can suck much more easily and get that all-important colostrum – the first milk the ewe produces. The colostrum has antibodies in it that protect the lamb in the early stages of its life,' Jenny's father explained. 'If a lamb can't get it naturally it has to be fed colostrum by bottle.'

Jenny nodded as she watched the lamb wobble precariously to its feet and start searching for its mother's teat. The ewe nudged her baby into place and the lamb began to suck, its tiny stub of a tail wagging furiously.

'I like feeding the orphaned lambs,' Jenny said, watching mother and baby.

'Let's hope we don't have too many of those this year,' Fraser Miles replied. 'I don't know how I'll manage if we do. There's more than enough work out here in the fields as it is.'

'I'll help,' said Jenny, looking up at her father.

Fraser Miles smiled down at her. 'It might come to that,' he said. 'But lambing is hard work, you know that.'

'I don't mind the hard work,' Jenny said.

'It's for Windy Hill, isn't it?'

Fraser Miles looked out over his land. 'It is, lass,' he agreed. 'It's all for Windy Hill – and worth it!'

Jenny was full of her news about Windy Hill's first lamb when she arrived at school. She met Carrie just as both girls turned into the playground on their bikes.

'That's marvellous,' Carrie enthused. 'I wish I'd seen it.'

'It *was* marvellous,' Jenny agreed, as they propped their bikes up in the bike shed, then walked across the yard as the bell rang for them to line up with their class, ready to go into school.

Ian Amery, Mrs Grace's nephew, was standing just in front of them, with his back to Jenny. He turned as they approached. Jenny was describing the tiny Blackface lamb to Carrie.

'Don't you ever think about anything else?' he asked Jenny.

'Sheep are important,' Jenny retorted.

'So you told me – yelled at me, I should say,' Ian said.

Ian was the same age as Jenny, and in the same class. He barely spoke to her which made Jenny feel alternately guilty and exasperated. Right now she felt exasperated. She had *tried* to apologise about the sheep incident. If he didn't want to be friends that was all right by her. He was a real bossyboots anyway.

'Mum wants to sketch Jess again,' Carrie put in hurriedly. 'The animal campaign people have asked for another illustration of him.'

'Wow!' breathed Jenny. 'They must really like Jess.'

'I don't see how anybody could like a lame dog,' said a voice behind Jenny.

Jenny turned round. Fiona McLay towered over her, looking down her nose. She was a lot taller than Jenny, though they were the same age. Jenny looked up at her, too angry to speak.

'He isn't lame,' Carrie retorted. 'He hardly limps at all.'

'He still *limps*,' declared Fiona, spitefully.

Fiona's little brother, Paul, stood beside her. '*I* like Jess,' he said stoutly. 'I think he's really brave.'

Jenny smiled at the little boy. Paul was seven.

He looked a little like his sister, but he was never bad-tempered like Fiona.

'Maybe you could come and visit Jess sometime,' Jenny offered. She spoke clearly, looking straight at Paul.

Paul had become deaf after a bad viral infection. But he was now a marvellous lip-reader, and Jenny always made sure she spoke directly to him.

'No, he can't,' Fiona snapped. 'Dad would never let Paul set foot on Miles land.'

Jenny's heart sank when she saw the disappointment on Paul's face as he lip-read his sister's words.

Ian flicked a cold look at Fiona. 'You like bird-watching don't you, Paul?' he asked, turning to Paul. 'I saw the report on the ringed plovers you did for the school noticeboard. It was really interesting.'

Paul flushed with pleasure and nodded eagerly. 'I got a gold star for it,' he said proudly.

'Hmmph!' said Fiona. 'I don't know why Paul is so keen on bird-watching. He can't even hear them.'

Jenny drew in her breath sharply. How could

Fiona say such a horrible thing? Luckily, Paul was still looking at Ian and didn't read the cruel words coming from Fiona's lips.

Ian turned round and looked full at Fiona, his green eyes full of anger, then he shifted his gaze back to Paul. 'I'll go bird-watching with you, Paul,' he said. 'I like it too, and I can describe all the bird calls to you.'

'Wow!' exclaimed the younger boy. 'Would you?'

Jenny looked at Ian in surprise. He was usually so brusque and unfriendly – at least to her. 'That's really nice of you, Ian,' she said.

Ian shrugged. 'It's no problem,' he said shortly. 'I'd enjoy it. And at least it's not sheep.'

Jenny rolled her eyes at Carrie. You just couldn't please some people no matter how hard you tried.

The bell rang and Fiona charged past Jenny and Carrie, pushing Paul towards his own line of classmates.

Carrie's face flushed. 'Of all the horrors!' she exclaimed. 'What has she got against Paul?'

Jenny thought for a moment. 'It's almost as if she's ashamed of having a deaf brother,' she said.

'Ugh! That's terrible!' Carrie declared.

'Is that you on your high horse again, Carrie?' Mrs Barker, their teacher, said as Jenny and Carrie walked past her into the classroom. 'You're always getting worked up about something.'

'Mum says I'm an activist,' Carrie told her, smiling.

Mrs Barker raised her eyebrows. 'Don't think I haven't noticed,' she said as the class settled down. 'Come to think of it, we're going to need some activists for the Graston common riding – or at least some active people.'

'When is the common riding committee going to choose the Graston Lass, Miss?' Fiona demanded from the back of the class.

Several of the boys groaned. Every year a girl from the senior class at Graston School was chosen as a sort of queen for the day. She had to ride at the head of the procession as it marked out the boundaries of the village. There was always a lot of excitement about who was going to be the Graston Lass – at least among the girls in the class. Fiona had been boasting for weeks that she was going to be chosen. After all, her father owned a good portion of the land around Graston.

'All you girls will get the opportunity to enter the competition when the time comes,' Mrs Barker said firmly, as Fiona flicked her hair into place, shaking her head back. The teacher continued: 'What I want you to think about in the meantime is the Graston Hero Prize. That's much more important.' She pointed to a box on the window ledge, saying, 'As most of you will know, the Graston Hero Prize is a prize that the common riding committee awards each year for things like bravery or community spirit. If you know of any examples of outstanding effort that should be rewarded you can submit your nomination to the committee. The box on the window ledge is there for your ideas.'

'I'd like to nominate little Paul for putting up with Fiona and for being so cheerful even though he's deaf,' Carrie whispered in Jenny's ear.

Jenny thought for a moment. 'I don't know if that would be a good idea,' she said at last.

'Why not?' asked Carrie indignantly.

'Because it might make Paul feel even more different,' said Jenny. 'I know it can't be easy for him being deaf but it doesn't seem right to give him a prize for it.'

Carrie's mouth dropped open and she shook her head. 'I never thought of that,' she said in wonder. 'You know, Jenny, you're really good at putting yourself in other people's shoes. I just go charging in like a bull in a china shop.'

Jenny grinned. 'You're an activist, remember?'

'And you're a – thoughtfulist,' Carrie added, giggling.

3

Jenny and Carrie stayed on for a while after school, discussing with Mrs Barker what they would do for the celebrations, so Jenny was a bit later than usual getting home. The first thing she saw as she cycled up the track was Matt's old motorbike parked in the farmyard. Jenny's face split into a smile. Matt was home! She hadn't been expecting him and that made it all the better.

Then Jenny saw Mercury. The big black horse was tethered to a ring on the stable wall. He whinnied as Jenny came through the gate and stamped his feet restlessly. Matt must have taken him out earlier. It was the first thing he did whenever he came home.

Jenny's smile disappeared and she gave the horse a wide berth. Mercury had been her mother's horse, the horse that had thrown and killed her. Fraser Miles had sold the animal immediately afterwards. But Matt had found Mercury at the Greybridge livestock market months later. The horse had been maltreated and Matt had bought him for next to nothing and brought him back to Windy Hill, much to Jenny's dismay. She couldn't understand how her father and Matt could stand having Mercury around after what the horse had done to her mother.

But Jenny's mood was instantly lifted when Jess came flying out of the farmhouse and launched himself at her in delight. Jenny scooped him up in her arms and gave him a cuddle. 'And what have you been up to today?' she asked him, burying her face in his fur.

The little dog licked her cheek, leaped out of her arms and ran round her feet, barking and wagging his tail furiously. Jenny laughed. 'Come on, let's go and see what Matt is doing home.'

Jenny dumped her bike against the wall and, together, they raced into the kitchen.

'Matt!' Jenny exclaimed, throwing herself at her brother. 'How come you're home?'

The tall, dark-haired young man caught her and swung her round. 'Hi, Jen,' he said, setting her back down on her feet. 'How are things?'

Jenny smiled up at him. 'Great now that you're here,' she enthused. 'I didn't know you were coming. How long are you staying?'

Matt ran a hand through his hair. It was a habit Fraser Miles had too and it made Matt look very like his father. 'I'm here for the lambing,' he said, grinning at his sister.

'*What*!' said Jenny. 'How? Why? That's great! *All* of the lambing?'

'Hey, slow down,' Matt said, laughing. 'Yes, I'm here until the lambing is done.'

'But how did you get away?' Jenny asked.

Matt grinned at her amazed face. 'It was easy,

really,' he said. 'I'm doing agriculture after all, and everybody on the course has to do a placement on a farm at some point in the year. As I've always intended to go into sheep farming, I put it to them at college that for my practical experience this year, I would come to Windy Hill to help with lambing. Of course, I'll have to study the books about lambing as well.'

'But that's brilliant, Matt,' Jenny enthused. 'And guess what! We had our first lamb today!'

'Really?' said Matt. 'In that case it looks as if I've arrived home just in time. Even *Dad* can't handle the lambing entirely on his own.'

Mrs Grace was standing by the Aga, stirring a pot on the stove. 'Your father *is* tired,' she agreed. 'And this is just the beginning of it. It's going to get much worse over the next few weeks. He doesn't have any of the extra workers this year, thanks to Calum McLay's dirty tricks.'

Matt gave her a reassuring smile. 'Don't worry, we'll pull through,' he said.

Jenny looked up at her brother's confident face. She only hoped he was right. She had been so worried about her father. But now

Matt was here, everything seemed better. She smiled in spite of her worries.

'Mercury isn't getting much exercise,' Mrs Grace informed Matt. 'Your dad doesn't have time for him.'

'I don't know where *I'll* find the time either,' Matt sighed. 'It's the lambing that's important at the moment.'

'Why don't you sell him?' Jenny asked.

Matt looked surprised. 'I couldn't do that,' he said. 'Anyway, he's still recovering. His physical injuries are better but it'll take him a while to get over his nervousness.'

Jenny clamped her mouth shut. Matt thought the world of Mercury and nothing she could say would change his mind about that.

'Ian rides,' Mrs Grace put in. 'He's a good horseman. He could exercise Mercury. I'm sure he'd love that.'

Matt looked thoughtful. 'I don't know about that, Ellen,' he said. 'Mercury can still be a little unpredictable.'

Jenny snorted. 'You mean dangerous, Matt,' she said.

Matt looked at her sympathetically.

'Look, Jen, I know you're a bit nervous of Mercury but that makes him even *more* nervous when you're around. You don't see him at his best.'

Jenny shook her head. 'How can you trust him?' she asked.

'That's the point,' said Matt. 'You've got to give trust to get it. You don't trust Mercury so you don't have his trust.'

Jenny shook her head. 'I'll never trust that horse – *never*!' she said.

Matt spread his hands out. 'So he'll never trust you,' he said.

'Why don't you try Ian out on Mercury?' Mrs Grace suggested. 'He's coming for tea. He should be here soon.'

'Good idea,' agreed Matt, making for the door. 'I'll just go and work off some of his energy before Ian arrives. I wouldn't want him to be too fresh for a new rider.'

Mrs Grace looked sympathetically at Jenny when Matt had gone. 'Your mother loved horses, you know,' she said. 'When we were girls she was always horse-mad. She used to jump the highest fences and walls.'

41

'I like horses too,' said Jenny. 'It's just Mercury I don't like – and I never will.'

Mrs Grace's face grew even more sympathetic. 'That's understandable,' she said. 'After what happened to your mother.'

'So why does Dad keep him?' Jenny asked.

Mrs Grace shrugged. 'Grief is a strange thing,' she said. 'Maybe Mercury reminds him of when your mother was alive.'

Jenny swallowed back the tears. 'He reminds me of how Mum died,' she said.

Mrs Grace was silent for a moment. 'Maybe you should tell your father that,' she said.

Jenny looked up at her, tears spilling over. 'I can't,' she said. 'He doesn't talk about her. You're the only one that ever talks about her to me.'

Mrs Grace didn't say anything else. She just held out her arms to Jenny and let her cry.

Ian arrived shortly afterwards but Jenny was in no mood to be friendly. Not that Ian made much of an effort.

'Why are your eyes so red?' he asked her.

Jenny glared at him. 'I've got an allergy,' she snapped, then blew her nose.

'So have I,' Ian replied. 'To rude people like you!'

'I wish you two could be friends,' Mrs Grace said, as Ian and Matt went out into the yard.

Jenny shrugged. 'Don't worry about it, Mrs Grace,' she replied. 'I don't care.'

'He'll come round,' Ellen Grace went on. 'He's always been stubborn.'

'Bossy!' corrected Jenny, as she and Mrs Grace followed them.

Matt handed Ian a riding-hat. 'That should fit,' he said. 'Now just take it easy to begin with. Walk him round the yard.'

Ian put one foot into the stirrup and hoisted himself into the saddle. He settled himself and ran a hand over Mercury's neck. The big horse whickered and Ian leaned forward, whispering in the horse's ear. Mercury's ears pricked but he still moved restlessly under Ian's weight.

Ian clicked his tongue. 'Walk on,' he said steadily to the horse. Mercury began to move forward, then stepped sideways, tossing his head. Ian gathered in the reins and brought the horse's head round. 'It's OK, boy,' he said. 'Walk on now.'

Jenny watched as Mercury moved forward again. Mrs Grace was right. Ian *was* good with horses.

'You're doing really well,' Matt congratulated the boy. 'Just keep him steady.'

But Mercury had other ideas. He didn't seem to like having a strange rider on his back. His big hoofs danced on the cobbles of the yard. Ian at once shortened the reins then let them out again almost immediately, deliberately confusing the horse to give himself time to get Mercury under control.

Jenny watched with interest. Ian was in no danger. Mercury was just testing him. Jenny had seen horses do this before. It was a battle of wills but she wasn't at all sure that Ian would win.

Jess suddenly ran forward and began to trot at Mercury's heels. Jenny was horrified – Jess might get trampled! She *had* to save him, but she just couldn't bring herself to go near the big horse. 'Jess!' she cried.

But Matt was already striding towards the puppy. However, he suddenly stopped and stood quite still, watching the two animals. 'Look at that,' he said.

Jenny *was* looking. Mercury had stopped dancing. He bent his head and Jess raised his. The two animals nuzzled each other, then Jess trotted calmly to the big horse's side and began to walk beside him. Mercury began to walk forward steadily with no sidestepping, and no skittishness.

'Jess is often in the stable with Mercury while you're at school, Jenny,' Mrs Grace said, coming to stand beside her. 'They're good friends.'

'But Mercury is *dangerous*,' said Jenny, appalled.

'Just a little nervous,' Matt corrected her. 'But just look at Jess. He's calmed Mercury right down.' Matt turned to face his sister. 'Jen, would you let Jess help with Mercury's training? Look how well they get on. Jess is herding Mercury.'

Jenny looked at Jess in amazement. Matt was right. Jess's sheepdog instincts were plain to see. He worked round Mercury's feet, keeping the horse steady. Jenny couldn't help but admire what Jess was doing but she was horrified at Matt's suggestion.

She couldn't possibly agree. This was the horse that had killed her mother. Then she saw

Matt's face. He didn't have time to train Mercury properly. He had to help their father and he was right. Jess *did* seem to calm Mercury down. If it could take some of the worry off Matt's shoulders how could she refuse?

'I'd certainly be happier with Jess along until Mercury gets used to me,' Ian said. 'The difference in Mercury with Jess at his heels is amazing.'

'I'd be happier too,' Mrs Grace told her nephew. 'I think you'd be a lot safer exercising Mercury with Jess on the job.'

Jenny looked at the others. They were all looking at her expectantly. She looked again at Jess. It was true. Mercury was as gentle as a lamb with Jess at her heels. The lambing, Jenny thought. That was what was important. Her father needed *all* the time Matt could spare. She swallowed.

'All right,' she said reluctantly. 'I don't have any choice, do I? But that doesn't mean I have to like it.'

4

Over the next few weeks, Ian was often at Windy Hill, exercising Mercury. Jenny still didn't like the idea but she found herself becoming interested in Mercury's progress. With Jess's influence, Mercury soon learned to tolerate Ian. Jenny was glad, however, when Ian was able to take Mercury out for rides on his own.

'You don't need Jess any longer, do you?' she

asked Ian on the first day of the Easter holidays. She was crossing the farmyard with a crate of babies' feeding-bottles filled with milk for the orphaned lambs.

Ian was in the yard, saddling Mercury, and Jess was sitting, watching the proceedings. Ian shook his head. 'Not really, but Jess enjoys being with us.'

'If you don't need him then you and Mercury can go out on your own,' Jenny said. 'I only agreed to let Jess help for a little while.'

Ian shrugged. 'Please yourself,' he said. 'Jess is your dog.'

'Yes he is,' agreed Jenny, as Ian mounted Mercury.

Jess rose at once to follow them but Jenny called him back. Jess looked round at her, puzzled.

'Here, Jess,' Jenny said firmly.

Jess trotted over to her and they both watched as Ian rode Mercury out of the yard. Jess whined a little and Mercury tried to turn his head but Ian kept the horse's head straight and didn't even turn round to wave goodbye.

'Come on, Jess,' Jenny said to the puppy.

'There's work to do. Let's go and see how the lambs are doing.'

Jenny and Jess made their way to the shearing shed where Fraser Miles had rigged up a lamb warmer for the newborn lambs whose mothers had died or rejected them. Sometimes a ewe had twins or triplets and couldn't care for all her lambs. Sometimes a ewe simply rejected her lamb and, if Mr Miles couldn't get another ewe to foster the lamb, then it had to be hand-reared for a few weeks.

The lamb warmer was a closed box with holes in the bottom and fan heaters underneath to blow warm air in. It was divided into two parts so that the lambs could be separated as Jenny fed each one. Every year there were a lot of lambs that had to be cared for in this way and Jenny loved looking after them.

She lifted the top of the box gently and, at once, the lambs scrambled towards her, lifting their little black faces and bleating piteously. There were almost thirty lambs in there. Jenny tickled the nearest lamb's nose and reached for a bottle. The lamb immediately opened his mouth and Jenny put the teat of the bottle between his lips, reaching at the same time for another bottle.

'I wish I had more than one pair of hands,' she said as the lucky lambs sucked greedily at their milk while the rest crowded round, eager for their turn.

'We all wish that at lambing time,' said a voice from the door.

Jenny turned her head. 'Hi, Dad,' she said. 'How are things going?'

Fraser Miles came over to stand beside her, looking down at the lamb warmer. 'I've had to bring six more lambs down,' he said. 'But none of these are ready to go out in the fields yet and there isn't room for any more in there.' He picked up a couple of bottles and began to help Jenny feed the lambs.

'What will you do with them?' Jenny asked.

'I guess I'll have to bring them into the kitchen,' Fraser said. 'I hope Ellen won't mind.'

'I'm sure she won't,' said Jenny, setting down the now empty bottles and picking up two more. 'And I can look after them just as well in the kitchen as here.'

THE CHALLENGE

51

Fraser smiled. 'You're doing a grand job with these, lass,' he said.

'I love doing it,' Jenny said, smiling. 'But I wish you'd let me help out in the fields as well. I've got time now that the Easter holidays have started. I could help you and still look after the lambs.'

The number of lambs had increased dramatically in the last week and Fraser was finding it difficult to cope. Jenny knew that the births would reach a peak soon and begin to tail off but, until then, the work would increase.

'It's hard work,' Fraser replied. 'It's hard enough for Matt and me, never mind a young girl. But I'll keep your offer in mind. I might just take you up on it if things get out of hand.'

Jenny looked at her father as he replaced his own empty bottles. 'That's good enough for me,' she told him. She allowed herself a small smile. She wouldn't push it. She knew her father too well to do that but she would remind him of what he had said, if things got really tough.

Jenny helped her father deposit the extra lambs in the kitchen before he headed back to the fields.

'Boxes,' said Mrs Grace. 'I'm sure I've got some that would do.'

'You don't mind them being in here, do you, Mrs Grace?' Jenny asked anxiously.

Ellen Grace smiled. 'Mind?' she said. 'I was brought up on a farm. When I was a girl we used to put the really small orphaned lambs in the Aga to warm them.'

'In the oven?' squeaked Jenny. 'You mean like cooking them?'

'Of course not.' Mrs Grace laughed. 'The oven was warm, not hot, and we left the door open. It was the quickest way to get very weak and tiny lambs warm,' Mrs Grace explained. 'Undersized lambs can get cold very quickly, and die. We didn't have lamb warmers in those days. Of course, most of the lambs were perfectly fine just laid around the oven in boxes. We can put these lambs around the Aga. That will be perfect for them.'

Jenny looked at Jess. 'How are you going to feel about that, Jess?' she asked. 'Your favourite spot is right in front of the Aga.'

But Jess took to the lambs very well. He even started herding them gently as Jenny put them down on the kitchen floor before transferring them to the prepared boxes.

'That should do it,' said Jenny as she popped the last lamb into its cosy cardboard box. She had lined the boxes with newspaper, just as she had done for Jess when he was an abandoned puppy.

Jess padded over to the nearest box and nuzzled it. At once a soft bleating came from inside and a small black nose peeked over the rim of the box. Jess sniffed and his tail began to wag. Then he went from box to box, sniffing each lamb in turn.

'He's saying hello,' said Jenny delightedly. 'He doesn't mind in the least losing his place in front of the Aga.'

'Just as well,' said Mrs Grace. 'Something tells me he won't get it back for a while!'

Mrs Grace was right. A week later, Jenny looked round the kitchen. There seemed to be orphaned lambs everywhere. Jess was curled up between two boxes, keeping a wary eye on the lambs. If any of them tried to climb out, Jess herded it back into its box.

'Poor little things,' Jenny said, as one lamb poked its head over the rim of a basket and bleated. 'But we haven't lost any of them.'

Mrs Grace smiled. 'That's because you've been looking after them so well, lass,' she said.

'I'm going to move another batch out of the lamb warmer later today,' Fraser Miles said from his seat at the kitchen table. He was snatching a quick bite to eat while Matt was working the top field. He and Matt tried to make sure that one of them was always with the ewes during daylight. 'We should be able to get some of these out of the kitchen.'

Jenny had taken the job of looking after the orphaned lambs very seriously and she knew her father was pleased with her work. It gave her such a thrill to see the little animals growing stronger by the day.

Just then Matt thrust his head round the kitchen door. His hair was standing on end and his face was flushed. 'Can you come, Dad?' he said to his father urgently.

'What's the matter?' his father asked sharply, standing up at once.

'It looks like a case of hypocalcaemia to me,'

Matt replied. 'But I'd rather you had a look.'

'What's that?' Jenny asked, worried.

'It's a deficiency in calcium,' Matt replied. 'It sometimes happens with pregnant ewes.'

Fraser Miles was already at the door, picking up his lambing bag from the dresser.

'Things have got really busy up in the top field,' Matt went on. 'I wish we had a bit more help.'

Jenny jumped down from the table. '*I* can help,' she said. Fraser hesitated a moment. 'You promised, Dad,' Jenny reminded him. 'You said you'd let me help if things got out of hand.'

'*Are* things getting out of hand up there, Matt?' Fraser Miles asked.

Matt grinned. 'I reckon we've reached peak lambing,' he said.

Fraser nodded. 'I'd call that out of hand,' he said. 'Come on, lass. Get your wellingtons and let's go.'

Though excited, Jenny cast a worried glance at the lambs.

'Don't worry about them,' Mrs Grace said. 'I'll make up their bottles and feed them if you aren't back in time.'

'Thanks, Mrs Grace,' Jenny said. She grabbed her wellingtons from the back porch and turned to Jess. 'Come on, boy.'

'No, Jenny,' said her father firmly. 'Jess can't come. He's a house dog.'

'But he's so good with the lambs,' Jenny protested. 'Look at him.'

Jess was gently nudging a tiny black lamb back into its basket. The little animal bleated but didn't try to climb out again.

'No arguments, Jenny,' her father said.

Jenny bit her lip as she followed Matt and her father out into the yard. The jeep's engine was running. Jess scampered out of the house. The puppy raised his head and howled as Jenny got in and the jeep drove off.

Jenny turned to look back. Mrs Grace had Jess by the collar to stop him running after the jeep. The housekeeper raised a hand and waved. Jenny waved back as the jeep turned up the track towards the top field. Poor Jess. He'd think she'd abandoned him, just as some of the ewes had abandoned their lambs.

She changed from trainers into her wellingtons as the jeep rattled along the rough farm track. Her father was looking worried. Jess would just have to put up with being left behind. The lambing was the important thing.

Matt drew the jeep to a halt beside the field gate. Jenny could see Jake and Nell amongst the flock, weaving their way in and out, keeping the ewes together.

Her father had already jumped out of the jeep, and now he was striding towards a ewe lying on the ground. The poor animal lay on her side, her body arched and her legs stiff. He kneeled down beside the ewe and opened his lambing bag.

'You were right, Matt, it is hypocalcaemia,' he said grimly. 'I'll need to give her an injection. Can you hold her head for me?'

Jenny watched as her father took a syringe and a bottle of clear liquid out of his bag. She had seen the lambing bag many times before. It was a sort of first-aid kit for sheep farmers. In it was fluid for marking the lambs with the Windy Hill symbol and penicillin in case the mother needed a quick injection to prevent infection. There was also lambing oil for the farmer to rub on his hands if he had to help ease the lamb out of the mother's body, and protein drinks for exhausted ewes. The bag itself was lined with soft sheep's wool so that if her dad had to transport a lamb into the house it wouldn't get cold.

Matt kneeled beside his father and made to take the ewe's head in his hands. Fraser Miles primed the syringe and examined it for air bubbles. There was a loud bleating and a flash of black and white as a sheepdog sped past them in pursuit of a ewe. Matt looked up.

'A bolter,' he said.

Jenny watched as Nell chased after the lumbering sheep.

'The ewe is making for the fence at the top,' she said.

Fraser Miles clicked his tongue. 'Get up there, Matt,' he said. 'That's Calum McLay's fence. It's in a bad state of repair and that ewe must be just about to give birth. Don't let her injure herself — or the lamb.'

Matt nodded and jumped to his feet, running across the short grass, whistling to Jake.

The other sheepdog sped to his side and

moved beside him like a shadow.

'I guess *you'd* better hold the ewe's head, Jenny,' Fraser Miles said.

Jenny crouched down, drawing the ewe's head on to her lap and stroking it. The animal's eyes had been closed but suddenly they opened and the sheep bleated weakly. Fraser Miles stretched a patch of skin on the sheep's flank and plunged the syringe home.

'Will she be OK?' Jenny asked, concerned.

Fraser Miles nodded. 'She should be,' he reassured her. 'We'll have to wait and see. The injection should take effect pretty quickly.'

The ewe's eyes were closed again, her body motionless. Jenny held her breath, willing the ewe to open her eyes, to get up. It wasn't just the ewe that was in danger. It was her unborn lamb as well.

The minutes seemed to drag by, then Jenny felt a shudder run through the ewe's body. The animal opened her eyes and began to struggle to her feet.

'Let her go,' Fraser told his daughter. 'But be ready to catch her if she bolts too.'

Jenny watched as the ewe scrambled to her

feet and began to crop the grass, pawing at the ground.

'It's amazing,' she breathed. 'A minute ago she seemed nearly dead.'

'I don't think it'll be long before her lamb is born,' Fraser said. 'Now, let's go and give Matt a hand.'

Jenny trudged up the field after him. As they approached Matt, her father turned to her and smiled. 'That was well done, Jenny,' he said. 'I was glad of your help.'

Jenny flushed with pride but one look at Matt's face told her something was wrong. Her brother was crouched beside the ewe, running his hands over her distended stomach.

'No wonder she bolted,' he said. 'I think it's a breech birth – and twins, too!'

Fraser dug into his lambing bag, drew out the bottle of lambing oil and rolled up his sleeves. 'Do you remember, lass?' he said to Jenny. 'Jess was a breech birth. That's when the baby animal is facing the wrong way in the womb,' he explained, as he rubbed the oil on his hands and forearms. 'Usually they're born head first, and, with twins, that's hard enough for a ewe. But with a breech birth the baby begins to come out backwards, and it can get stuck. So the ewe is going to need my help to ease the lamb out.'

Matt stationed himself at the ewe's head as Fraser got down on his knees and began to examine the ewe. Suddenly the animal began to bleat pitifully and strain against Matt. Matt had his work cut out holding on to her. The poor thing wanted to get away from the pain of imminent birth and the only way she knew how was to bolt.

'Here it comes,' said Fraser Miles. 'Get ready to take it, Jenny.'

Jenny watched, fascinated, as her father eased the little creature into the world. Tiny back legs appeared first, encased in the birth sac. Fraser moved his hands, supporting the little body as it emerged from its mother's womb.

'Push again, old girl,' Matt whispered to the ewe.

As if she had heard him, the ewe gave an almighty push and Fraser Miles was suddenly holding a slippery newborn lamb. He looked at it for a moment and Jenny watched his face.

All the usual worry and seriousness had gone. Her father must have delivered a thousand lambs, but he looked as if this was the very first one he had seen. Jenny understood more than ever before how important sheep farming was to him.

The ewe bleated and began to strain again.

'And here comes the other one,' Fraser said, handing the warm, wet lamb to Jenny. 'Put this one down beside his mother,' he said. 'The sooner she starts licking him clean the better.'

Jenny took the little lamb in her arms and laid him gently beside the ewe. Almost at once the lamb tried to get to his feet, bumping blindly into his mother's side. Jenny guided him towards the ewe's head but the ewe was already giving birth to the other twin.

'This one is the right way round,' Fraser said triumphantly. 'That's it girl – steady now.'

The second lamb slid easily on to the grass and the ewe shook her head and stopped bleating. Jenny's lamb nuzzled at his mother's neck and the ewe turned to him. As Jenny watched, the mother began to lick her lamb, cleaning him and stimulating his circulation.

Then she nudged him towards her flank. Jenny smiled as the tiny lamb searched for what instinct told him he needed.

'Can I give him a hand? He doesn't know how to feed,' she said.

'Better not,' said Matt. 'Sheep often reject lambs if you interfere too much.'

As Jenny watched, the little lamb at last found what he was looking for and fastened on his mother's teat, sucking furiously.

'I think he's going to be all right,' said Jenny.

'Here's the other one,' Fraser said, laying the second lamb in front of its mother.

'The ewe has got the hang of it too,' said Matt as the ewe began to lick her second lamb. 'I think we can leave them to it.'

'Isn't it wonderful?' breathed Jenny.

Fraser Miles took a rough towel out of his bag and wiped his arms.

'I feel that, every time I see a lamb born,' he said. 'But it's hard work.'

'Oh, I wouldn't mind that,' said Jenny seriously. 'I mean, what could be better than helping lambs to be born?'

Fraser looked at his daughter seriously for a

moment. 'You really believe that, don't you, Jenny?'

Jenny nodded, equally serious. 'I love the farm and I love the sheep,' she said. 'Windy Hill is just the best place in the world.'

Fraser turned away and looked out over the fields to the sea beyond. 'You're right, lass,' he said. 'And we'll hang on to it, I promise you that.'

Jenny looked at the twin lambs snuggled close to their mother. Everything she loved was here on this farm.

'What's next?' she asked stoutly.

Matt grinned. 'Talk about a glutton for punishment. Come on, Jenny. There's *plenty* to be done.'

5

From then on, Jenny divided her time between looking after the orphaned lambs and helping her father and Matt in the fields. She was up at first light every morning to give the lambs their feeds, then handed them over to Mrs Grace when she arrived. Matt usually popped back into the farmhouse to collect her and take her back with him.

Every so often, he arrived with new

abandoned or orphaned lambs. He would then collect some of the stronger lambs from the lamb warmer, leaving Jenny to divide the new arrivals between the lamb warmer and the kitchen. Jenny selected the lambs she thought needed the extra attention they could get in the farmhouse and separated them from those that could safely be put in the lamb warmer.

'I'm off back up to the top field, Jenny,' Matt told her, one morning. 'I'll come back for you in a couple of hours, all being well.'

Jenny waved goodbye to her brother. The back of the jeep was full of lambs that were ready to go back into the fields. They bleated piteously, tumbling over one another but Jenny knew they were fit to be outdoors now. There were always new lambs to replace them.

'Come on, Jess,' she said. 'Let's get these lambs settled.' But Jess was already hard at work, herding the tiny lambs into a corner of the kitchen.

Jenny was carrying a boxful of lambs out to the lamb warmer when Ian came out of the stables. He must have been exercising Mercury.

Jenny hadn't known he was around. She'd been far too busy with the lambs.

'Want a hand?' Ian asked as she passed him.

Jenny hesitated. She and Ian didn't get on but right now she reckoned Windy Hill needed all the help it could get.

'Sure,' she said. 'There's another box of lambs to come out to the lamb warmer. Can you fetch it?'

Ian nodded and strode off towards the house. Moments later, he joined her in the shearing shed and handed the box of lambs to her.

'Aren't they great?' he said, peering into the lamb warmer.

'I thought you didn't like sheep,' Jenny said.

'I never said that,' Ian replied. 'You accused me of not knowing anything about sheep – which I don't. But I could always learn.'

Jenny looked at him. 'Are you serious?' she asked. 'Because, if you are, there's a mountain of work you could help with.'

Ian grinned, suddenly looking much more friendly. 'Try me,' he said.

Jenny smiled back. 'Oh, don't worry, I will,' she told him.

★ ★ ★

Mrs Grace was looking round the kitchen in mock despair as Jenny and Ian came back into the house. 'This lot is going to keep you busy,' she said, shaking her head. 'I'll get the bottles ready.'

'Ian's going to help,' Jenny said.

'So he told me when he came for those lambs,' Mrs Grace replied. 'Well, you know what they say – many hands make light work.'

Jenny and Ian began filling boxes with fresh straw and tucking up the tiny lambs warmly. By the time they had finished Mrs Grace had lined up a row of bottles for them. The kitchen was filled with the sound of bleating.

'Where do I start?' asked Ian.

'Just pick a couple of lambs and do as I do,' Jenny told him. 'Look, I'll show you.'

'I'd help but I've got to get on with cleaning the house,' Ellen Grace apologised. 'After all, the humans need looking after too.'

'You've been great, making up the bottles, Mrs Grace,' Jenny called, as the housekeeper went upstairs. 'We'll manage.'

Jenny scooped up two bottles. She

approached a box with two lambs in it, inserting the rubber teats into the little animals' hungry mouths. She smiled as she felt the tug on the bottles. The lambs were so tiny but they would soon be strong enough to go back to the fields.

'That's all you do, Ian,' she said.

There was a scampering sound and Jenny turned round. Ian was chasing after a lamb that was skittering across the kitchen floor

'It got away,' Ian said, flushing, as the lamb staggered under the kitchen table on its wobbly little legs. 'I didn't want to grab it too hard and it slid out of my hands.'

'They're stronger than you think,' Jenny reassured him. 'You won't hurt it if you pick it up firmly.' She turned and whistled to Jess. The puppy leaped up and shot under the table after the lamb. A moment later the tiny creature teetered out, Jess behind it.

'That'll do, Jess,' Jenny said as Ian bent to pick up the lamb. Jess immediately moved back and lay down but he didn't take his eyes off the lamb.

'That's what shepherds say to their dogs,' Ian

said, tucking the lamb under his arm and picking up a bottle.

Jenny nodded. 'Jess knows all the commands,' she told him. 'I taught him right from the start.'

'It's a pity he couldn't be a working dog,' Ian said. 'But if he had been you wouldn't have had him as a pet.'

'I'd much rather have Jess as a pet,' she agreed. 'But Dad says maybe some day he'll sire pups that will be working dogs.'

Ian smiled. 'That would be great,' he said.

Jenny looked up, surprised. Maybe Ian wasn't so bad after all.

Ian looked round the kitchen. 'Are there usually this many orphaned lambs?'

Jenny shook her head. 'Not usually,' she said. 'But there have been a lot of premature births and a few other complications. We've lost more ewes than we normally do. Dad thinks it's because of the fright the ewes had when they got out of the cliff field.'

'Look,' said Ian. 'Can we just forget that? I mean, you know it wasn't my fault.'

Jenny frowned. At first she had blamed Ian for letting the ewes out, but on further investigation it had looked as if Calum McLay had been the culprit except there was no way of proving it. 'You mean start again?' she said.

Ian nodded. 'If you like.'

'We could try,' said Jenny doubtfully. 'But don't go bossing me around.'

'Fair enough,' Ian replied. They both smiled.

A tiny lamb scrabbled at the side of his box, overturning it. The little creature tottered towards Jenny on thin, spindly legs.

'Oh, do you want milk too?' Jenny said. She transferred both bottles to one hand and reached for another, holding it out to the escaped lamb. The lamb fastened on it eagerly, then collapsed on the floor in a heap.

Jenny giggled and positioned the bottle so that the lamb could continue sucking. Her other two lambs were protesting at the awkward position of *their* bottles. Jenny turned back to them. 'Hurry now,' she whispered. 'There are lots more to feed.'

There was a bleating behind her and Jenny turned her head. The bottle of milk had rolled away from the other lamb's reach and the poor thing was trying to stand. He kept collapsing again on his weak little legs.

Suddenly Jess darted forward and gently rolled the bottle back towards the tiny lamb. The animal fastened on to it again, closing his eyes with pleasure as he sucked on the teat.

'Good boy, Jess!' Jenny congratulated him.

'Look at that!' said Ian. 'Now there are three of us feeding the lambs. It's a pity Jess can't help out like that in the fields. Matt was telling me that some of the lambs aren't getting enough nourishment and they might die.'

Jenny nodded. 'Even lambs in the fields sometimes need extra feeding,' she said. 'But, without more help, we just can't get round them all.'

'I could help out there too,' Ian offered.

But Jenny was watching Jess. 'Ian,' she said. 'Do you think we could rig up a harness for Jess and attach a couple of baby bottles to it?'

'What for?' Ian asked.

'I've just had the most marvellous idea,' Jenny said, excitedly. 'We could make some kind of harness so that Jess could carry milk to the weaker lambs. If Dad could see Jess doing that

I'm sure he'd let him help in the fields,' she explained.

Jenny and Ian finished feeding the lambs in the kitchen while Jenny outlined her idea, trying to think of the simplest way of making a harness.

'We could try straps,' said Ian.

Jenny frowned. 'They might get caught on the fences.'

'What about an old waistcoat?' suggested Ian after a moment.

Jenny tried to picture it in her mind. 'You know, Ian,' she said. 'I think that just might work.'

An old waistcoat of Fraser's made a terrific harness once they had taken in the back. Jenny cut holes in the bottoms of the pockets.

'There,' she exclaimed. 'The waistcoat goes round Jess's middle and the bottles slide into the pockets. It's perfect. Jess can take milk to the lambs in the fields – one bottle on each side.'

'And you think it'll work?' Ian asked doubtfully.

'It's *got* to work,' Jenny said determinedly.

'Dad just *can't* afford to lose any more lambs.'

At that moment Mrs Grace came back downstairs and stared at Jess. Jenny explained what they were doing.

The housekeeper shook her head. 'Well, well,' she said. 'I've seen a lot of things in my time but I reckon this beats the lot.'

There was a sound in the yard outside and Jenny whirled round. 'That'll be Matt. He said he'd come back for me.'

Mrs Grace took off her apron. 'I'm coming to have a look too,' she decided. 'I wouldn't miss this for the world!'

'What on earth are you doing with Jess out here?' thundered Fraser Miles as Matt stopped the jeep at the edge of the top field. Jenny winced but she was determined.

'Just let her show you her idea, Fraser,' Mrs Grace suggested.

Fraser Miles looked as if he was going to say no, but Mrs Grace was so calm and reasonable that he nodded reluctantly.

'If that dog upsets the ewes you'll be in trouble, Jenny,' he warned.

'He won't, Dad,' she assured him. 'Just give him a chance.' Jenny led Jess to where two lambs lay side by side, their eyes closed.

'I tried to set those two on to another ewe after their mother rejected them,' Matt said. 'It didn't work. The poor things don't stand a chance.'

Jenny knew that 'setting on' was when a sheep farmer covered a lamb with the skin of a stillborn or dead lamb. That way the mother of the dead lamb might be persuaded to think it was her own lamb, and feed it.

'Those were too weak even to bring into the house,' Fraser added.

Jenny looked down at the lambs. They lay side by side, their eyes closed, hardly breathing. 'Come, Jess,' she said softly.

Gently moving the lambs a little she made room for Jess to lie down between them. As the sheepdog pup nestled his body into place, he began to lick the lambs. Jenny held her breath as first one and then the other lamb opened its eyes.

'At least they're still alive,' she breathed.

She manoeuvred the bottles of milk into

place, lifting the lambs' heads towards the teats. For a moment she thought the lambs were too weak to suck, then she noticed one of them squirming closer to Jess's warm body. The little lamb lifted its head and fastened on the teat. Then he began to suck.

Jess lay perfectly still as Jenny repeated the procedure with the other lamb. But this other one was much weaker.

'You're wasting your time, Jenny,' Fraser Miles said to her gently. 'That one will never make it.'

Jenny looked sadly down at the lamb. It lay quite still, its eyes closed. As she watched she saw a tremor run through its body, then it lay motionless again.

She looked up at her father. 'It's dead, isn't it?' she asked.

Fraser nodded. 'I told you that pair were too far gone.'

Jenny felt a lump in her throat. Not only was the little lamb dead, but her father would ask her to take Jess away.

'This one isn't,' said Matt. 'Look at him.'

Matt was right. The other lamb was sucking

gustily at the bottle of milk. Suddenly it lifted its head and bleated, then, exhausted, it lay down. Jess moved, shifting the bottle nearer the lamb's mouth and Fraser Miles laughed.

'That pup is actually trying to feed the lamb,' he said. 'I've never seen anything like it.'

'That's what I wanted to show you,' Jenny said eagerly. 'I can strap two bottles at a time on Jess and he can feed the lambs here in the fields. The kitchen is full and so is the lamb warmer – but Jess can help out here.'

Fraser Miles scratched his head. 'I don't know about that,' he said.

The lamb finished the milk in the bottle and lay back. Matt picked him up and Jess scampered away. Jenny watched the pup. He nosed around the ewes until he found an abandoned lamb, lay down and began the procedure all over again with the unused milk bottle.

Matt held the lamb close to his chest. 'I reckon Jess has just saved one lamb,' he said. 'And look at him – he's doing it again.'

'Well . . .' said Fraser, clearly bemused. 'I've just never come across anything like this.'

Ellen Grace smiled. 'There's a first time for everything, Fraser,' she said. 'And if you take my advice – go with it. After all, if it works, why not?'

Fraser rubbed his forehead. 'I must admit, I'd be glad of any help at the moment,' he said. 'OK, Jenny, that dog has got a job to do. But if he even *looks* like upsetting the ewes he's out. Understand?'

Jenny nodded, her eyes shining. 'I understand,' she said. 'But he won't. He'll be such a help. You'll see.'

'Hmmph!' said her father but Jenny was watching his eyes. Fraser Miles was looking at Jess with a new respect.

6

Jenny was so busy working with Jess she hardly noticed the time passing. Matt had run the jeep down to the farm, taking Mrs Grace back and bringing up a churn of milk to fill the bottles. Mrs Grace had insisted that they return to the house for a bite to eat at lunchtime, and they had taken it in turns to do so: Jenny going first with Matt, and Ian going with Fraser afterwards. Even so, they had all been back in the fields by one o'clock and had been hard at work ever since.

Later that afternoon, Jenny stopped to look at her watch. 'Almost five o'clock, Jess,' she said. 'I'm getting hungry again!'

Jess had been working tirelessly, seeking out lambs in danger. Even her father was impressed. He and Matt were up at the far end of the top field now. Ian was with them, learning about lambing and loving it.

Jenny smiled. Calum McLay might have made sure that her father couldn't afford to outbid him for casual workers but now Fraser had Matt, Ian and Jenny – and Jess – to help him.

'We're going to beat you yet, Mr McLay,' Jenny whispered under her breath. 'Your dirty tricks haven't worked after all.' She looked down at her puppy. 'Isn't it wonderful, Jess? I can work in the fields *and* have you with me.'

Jess barked and wagged his tail and Jenny looked towards the top field. She could make out two figures up there, moving amongst the ewes. She saw Nell flowing like a shadow in and out of the flock, her distinctive white ears clearly visible. But where was Jake?

Jenny cast around her. Jake was an outrunner. Sheepdogs were usually one of two types. Nell was the kind of sheepdog that worked best close in to the sheep, controlling them with her eyes, outstaring them and making them do as she wanted. Jake was the other kind. He could run for miles, rounding up the flock and driving them where the shepherd wanted them to go. An outrunner was absolutely essential on a farm like theirs with its hilly terrain. Like all outrunners, Jake had excellent hearing. He could hear her father whistle from half a mile away.

Jenny screwed up her eyes, searching the top field. Maybe her father had sent the dog out to round up a batch of stray ewes. But, if so, her father would be standing straight, intent on his dog, whistling his instructions to it. But Jenny could see that Fraser Miles was crouched low over the bulk of a ewe. Clearly he was busy with a difficult birth. Ian was with him, also bending down. Matt was even further away, attending to another ewe. And still there was no sign of Jake.

Jenny pursed her mouth and whistled, then she scanned the fields once more but no black and white shape responded to her call. She frowned, trying to remember when she had last seen Jake. It must have been around lunchtime, but she'd been so busy since that she hadn't noticed if he'd passed through the field she was working in.

Jenny turned to Jess. The sheepdog puppy was standing, legs stiff and nose pointing over the hill towards the McLay farm. His ears were pricked, every sense alert. Jenny looked at him thoughtfully. Had he heard something she hadn't?

She whistled again, but this time she watched Jess. He turned briefly towards her, but he knew Jenny would never whistle for him while he was standing so close to her. Jess turned back, his nose still pointing in the same direction, towards the McLay farm, then he gave a short, sharp bark.

Jess had definitely heard something that was beyond human range of hearing. Jenny wondered what to do. Her father, Matt and Ian were all obviously very busy.

Jenny made up her mind. If Jake was in trouble then it was up to her and Jess to find out.

She bent down to the puppy. 'Jake,' she said urgently to the little dog. 'Find Jake, Jess.'

Jess looked up at her, his head on one side.

'*Jake*,' Jenny repeated insistently.

At once Jess dropped his head and began to move across the field. Jenny followed him, her heart hammering. Stumbling over the field, she went after Jess up the hill towards the stile that led to the adjoining field, the one that bordered Calum McLay's land. It seemed much farther than she remembered, she thought, as she crossed the stile and dropped into the next field.

Then, at last, she came in sight of the boundary. Ahead she could see the fence her father had been worried about. One section of it gleamed, shining in the rays of the sun. Jenny frowned. That whole fence had been old and rusty. Part of it shouldn't be shining like that. Then her attention was caught by a dark shape lying beside the fence.

Jess had seen it too and was running towards it. Jenny hurried after him. Maybe it was just a patch of mud, she told herself. But even as she tried to tell herself that, she knew it wasn't true. She recognised that shape. She recognised the white pattern within the black that she could now see as she drew closer. It was the white patch on Jake's chest. It was Jake – and he was lying as still as death.

Jenny raced the last twenty metres towards the dog. Her legs jarred on the uneven ground beneath her feet, and her heart thumped with the effort of putting on one last spurt. Then she was there. She threw herself down beside the sheepdog, struggling for breath.

Jess had already reached Jake. The puppy was licking the older dog's face. As Jenny put her hand out to touch Jake, Jess lifted his head and howled.

Jake opened his eyes at the sound, and tried to move. Then he gave a soft whine and slumped back. Jenny gasped with relief. At least he wasn't dead. She ran her hand along his flank, then cried out when her hand came away covered in blood.

More gently, she parted the dog's thick coat. It was matted with blood and there was an old piece of barbed wire caught in the skin of the dog's side. 'Oh, Jake,' Jenny gasped.

She looked at the new piece of fencing, puzzled. Why had Calum McLay replaced only one small section of the old and dangerous barbed-wire fence? And when had he done it?

But that would have to be dealt with later. Jake was badly injured and there was no time to lose. Jenny looked at Jess. 'Stay!' she commanded.

Jess lay down close to Jake as Jenny got to her feet and sped back the way she had come. Behind her Jess let out another howl but Jenny knew he would stay with the injured dog. She had to get help as quickly as possible.

The breath rasped in her throat as Jenny pounded down the hill. She scrambled on to the stile that connected the two fields and stood on top of it, shouting and waving. Nell looked up and moved towards her. Then Fraser Miles turned and began to run towards her, closely followed by Matt and Ian. Jenny jumped down from the stile and ran on, her legs weak under her, stumbling on the rough ground.

Matt was the first to reach her. 'What's wrong?' he yelled.

Jenny collapsed into his arms. 'It's Jake,' she gasped breathlessly. 'He's hurt . . . The boundary fence in the far field . . . Jess is with him.'

Fraser Miles arrived and looked at her. 'How badly hurt?' he asked.

'Pretty badly, I think,' Jenny answered. 'There's a lot of blood – and barbed wire.'

Fraser Miles's mouth set in a tight line. 'Get the jeep up, Matt,' he said. 'Bring it round by the other gate. We'll take Jake directly to Tom Palmer.' Then he whistled to Nell and started to run across the field towards the stile.

Matt looked at Jenny. 'Are you all right?' he asked.

Jenny nodded. 'Go on,' she gasped out. 'I'll follow when I've got my breath back.'

'I only hope Tom Palmer is there,' Matt said anxiously. Mr Palmer was the local vet.

Ian caught his arm. 'I'll run down to the farm and ring him,' he said. 'I'll get him on his mobile and make sure he's ready for you.'

Matt ran a hand through his hair. 'It's a long way back to the house,' he said.

'I used to do cross-country running at my last school,' Ian reassured him. 'Anyway, Jenny can't run all that way. She's done enough already.'

'She certainly has,' agreed Matt. 'OK, Ian, get going. Jenny, get back to Jake and we'll drop you and Jess off at the road end.'

Jenny nodded as Ian turned and began to run down the hill towards the farmhouse. It *was* a long way but he was covering the ground well.

Jenny sank to the ground and watched Matt, running long-legged down the field towards the jeep. Her heartbeat steadied and she began to get her breath back. She saw her father disappear over the brow of the hill and got to her feet, her legs still a little shaky.

Doggedly, she began to walk back the way she had come. Her steps were heavy. She couldn't get the picture of Jake out of her mind. He had looked so bad and there had been so much blood. She felt tears thick in her throat and took a deep breath. Crying wouldn't help. If Jake died, her father would have enough to worry about without her being upset.

Head up, she began to stride towards the stile. As she clambered over it, the wind caught her hair and lifted it from her face. She looked out over the farm towards the sea. Jake was part of Windy Hill. He *had* to be all right.

'Drink this and you'll feel better,' Mrs Grace said to Jenny.

Jenny looked up at the housekeeper and warmed her hands on the steaming mug of cocoa. She and Ian were sitting at the big kitchen table in the farmhouse. Matt had dropped her off at the end of the road and Ian had managed to get in touch with Tom Palmer. All she and Ian and Mrs Grace could do now was wait.

'They should be home soon,' Ian said as Jenny took a sip of cocoa.

'It might take a little time,' Ellen Grace warned him. 'And, don't forget, those lambs will be needing another feed soon.'

Jenny smiled weakly. 'We won't forget,' she said. She smiled at Ian. 'Thanks for today,' she said.

Ian smiled back. 'Any time,' he replied. 'I really enjoyed working with the sheep. I just wish Jake hadn't been hurt. It was lucky you found him.'

'It was Jess that found him,' Jenny said.

Jess was curled up asleep between two lambs. He had wanted to go with Jake to the vet and had howled as the jeep drove off. Poor Jess. He knew something was wrong.

'Tom Palmer is a good vet, Jenny,' Mrs Grace said comfortingly.

Jenny nodded. 'I know. He looked after Jess's leg. He'll do his very best for Jake. He knows how important Jake is to Dad.'

Ellen Grace gave Jenny a hug. 'And meanwhile,' she said briskly, 'there's one thing to remember about living on a farm – you're never short of a job to take your mind off your worries. There's a lot of lambs around here who would be grateful for a feed!'

Jenny smiled. Mrs Grace was right. Moping wouldn't help but feeding the lambs would! She and Ian finished their cocoa and started making up the bottles.

When the jeep turned into the yard Jenny looked up, surprised. It was later than she had thought. Feeding the lambs really had taken her mind off Jake for a while.

Her father and Matt came into the kitchen together. Jenny swallowed. Jake wasn't with them.

'Is he . . . ?' Jenny couldn't finish the sentence.

Fraser Miles reached out and ruffled her hair. 'He's going to be all right,' he reassured her.

Jenny let out a huge sigh of relief.

'But you haven't brought him home,' Ian said.

'Tom operated on him straight away,' Matt explained. 'The barbed wire was embedded quite deep, and the wound was inflamed. It'll be a while before he recovers.'

Ellen Grace looked worried. 'What about the lambing?' she asked. 'How will you manage without him?'

Fraser Miles sat down heavily at the table. 'We'll have to do the best we can with Nell,' he sighed.

'I can't understand how it happened,' Matt said.

'Jake was probably trying to rescue a stray ewe from McLay land,' Fraser guessed.

Matt frowned. 'But there was no gap in the fencing just there. In fact, a section of fencing had been repaired.'

Fraser looked at his son. 'When I passed by that section of fencing yesterday it was still broken and rusting,' he said, gravely. 'A sheep, still with its thick winter coat, would be protected against the wire as it pushed its way through. But Jake was unlucky. And,' Fraser concluded, 'I'd be willing to bet that the broken section of fence was replaced with a new section *after* Jake got caught in it. Sheep farmers usually keep a spare roll of wire fencing in the back of their truck,' he explained. 'It wouldn't have taken McLay long to replace that small section, so that he couldn't be blamed for having a dangerous fence.'

Jenny gasped. 'But if the fence was fixed *after* Jake was injured that means somebody just left Jake lying there, hurt! Somebody repaired the fence and ignored him!'

'Surely nobody would do a thing like that?' protested Ellen Grace.

'Nobody with any decency,' said Fraser Miles. 'But if Calum McLay wanted to hide the fact that it was his old fence that caused the injury—'

'Of course,' Matt broke in. 'We can't prove a thing. McLay could say he had already repaired the fence – that he'd never seen Jake.'

'Exactly,' said Fraser.

Jenny laid a hand on her father's arm. She was longing to ask him why Calum McLay had such a grudge against him but one look at his grey, exhausted face was enough. Now wasn't the time for questions like that. 'Jess and I will help,' she offered.

'And so will I,' Ian put in.

Fraser Miles smiled. 'Thanks for the offers,' he said. 'You two will be a good help. But you know how I feel about Jess, Jenny. He isn't a sheepdog. He did really well with his bottles of milk, but he can't replace Jake.'

'Maybe not,' said Matt briskly. 'But he's all we've got. We might be glad of him.'

Fraser Miles shook his head. 'I'm tired,' he confessed. 'I suppose you might be right, Matt. Goodness knows we couldn't be any worse off than we are now.'

Jenny's head came up. 'You said we'd hang

on to Windy Hill – no matter what,' she declared. 'You promised.'

Fraser Miles flushed. 'And I meant it, Jenny,' he said. 'You're right. Of course we'll get through this.'

Jess woke up and began to round up a couple of stray lambs that had escaped from their boxes. Jenny saw her father's face relax as he watched the pup.

'And Jess will do his best to help,' she said softly.

'That's all any of us can do, lassie,' Fraser replied.

Jenny didn't say anything more. She just hoped their best was good enough.

7

Jenny was reluctant to go back to school at the end of the Easter break. Normally she liked school – apart from the hassle she got from Fiona McLay – but she wouldn't be able to help her father as much as she had been doing, and neither would Ian. Fraser and Matt would have to cope.

'They'll manage,' Carrie comforted her as they took their places in class and got out their maths workbooks. 'After all, the peak of the lambing is over. It's gone well, hasn't it?'

Jenny smiled. 'They've had a hundred and forty per cent yield so far,' she said.

'What does that mean?' asked Carrie.

'Well, from eight hundred of our ewes, we've got about eleven hundred lambs. But there are still around two hundred ewes waiting to give birth,' Jenny answered.

Carrie's jaw dropped. 'Wow!' she said. 'That's an awful lot of lambs.'

'Dad was hoping to get closer to a hundred and fifty per cent yield by the end of the lambing,' Jenny replied. 'That would mean a yield of fifteen hundred lambs, but I don't think he can do that without Jake. Sheepdogs can help such a lot, picking out ewes in distress and rounding them up for the farmer, so he can help the sheep to deliver their lambs safely.'

'How *is* Jake?'' asked Carrie.

Jenny smiled. 'He's recovering,' she told her friend. 'But he's still weak. He lost a lot of blood and he needed quite a few stitches. He can't understand why he can't be out in the fields with Nell. Poor Jake.'

'But Jess is helping,' Carrie went on.

'He's doing his best,' Jenny agreed. 'But he's no substitute for Jake. Dad's right. There's a big difference between a working dog and a house dog.'

Carrie looked at Jenny sympathetically. 'It'll work out all right, you'll see.'

Jenny nodded. Carrie usually managed to cheer her up but this time it didn't seem to be working.

'The selection for the Graston Lass will be on Saturday in the village hall,' Mrs Barker announced from the front of the class.

There were excited murmurs among the girls and Carrie turned to Jenny. 'We'll go together,' she said.

Jenny shook her head. 'I can't,' she explained. 'Dad needs me on the farm. I can't let him down.'

'You wouldn't be chosen anyway,' said a voice behind them and Jenny turned to see Fiona McLay leaning over her desk. She must have been listening to every word they said.

Carrie stuck her chin out. 'Says who?' she demanded, sticking up for her friend.

'I can't come to the selection anyway,' Jenny said. 'It doesn't matter.'

'Poor little good girl,' Fiona mocked. 'She has to help her dad on the farm. Some sheep farmer that needs a girl to help him.'

Carrie leaned across Fiona's desk. 'And I suppose you think you're going to be the Graston Lass?' she said.

Fiona shrugged and tucked her hair back. 'Why not?' she replied confidently. 'Who else do you think they'll choose? Not you anyway. You're an incomer. You only moved here last year.'

Carrie looked as if she was going to explode and Jenny laid a hand on her arm. 'Leave it, Carrie,' she urged.

Carrie looked at Jenny's pale face and her angry expression subsided. 'OK,' she said. 'Fiona isn't worth arguing with anyway.'

This time it was Fiona's turn to flush. 'What do you mean by that?' she almost shouted.

'Quieten down at the back,' Mrs Barker called. 'Where is your maths workbook, Fiona? We're nearly ready to start . . .'

★   ★   ★

Fraser Miles always tried to come into the house for a quick cup of tea when Jenny got back from school. Jenny would have a snack and then spend a couple of hours helping him until it got dark.

That afternoon both he and Matt were there. Jenny took that as a good sign. Things weren't quite as hectic as they had been two weeks ago. Matt was slumped comfortably in an armchair and her father watched Jenny as she sat with Jake in front of the Aga. His side was still heavily bandaged but his temperature had gone down a lot and the infection seemed to be under control. Jess was curled up beside the bigger dog as they both snoozed in front of the stove.

'Jake owes his life to you, lass,' Fraser said to her. 'Tom reckoned that if he'd lost any more blood he wouldn't have been able to save him.'

Jenny looked up from her position beside the dogs. The sheepdog was in the farm kitchen for the duration of his convalescence. Even Fraser had agreed that Jake needed extra warmth and comfort while he recovered. 'It was Jess that led me to him,' she said.

Jess stirred in his sleep and Jenny put her

hand out, smoothing his ears. He snuffled and half woke, licking her hand.

'It seems a pity to disturb him,' Mr Miles said. 'Do you want to have a break this afternoon, Jenny?'

Jenny grinned. 'Are you trying to get rid of us, Dad?' she asked. 'I was only waiting for Ian to arrive. I don't need a break.'

Right at that moment there was the sound of bicycle wheels on the cobbles outside. 'That sounds like him now,' said Fraser.

'Let's go then,' said Jenny, rising to her feet.

Matt laughed. 'You're a slave driver, Jen,' he accused her. 'I was just getting comfortable.'

Jenny grinned. Matt might sound as if he was complaining but he got up quickly enough and made his way to the door.

As they approached it, the door opened and Ian came in. 'Ready?' he said.

'Just waiting for you,' said Jenny. 'Where have you *been*?'

Ian grinned as Jess jumped up and ran to him, wagging his tail. 'You could have gone without me,' he said.

Jenny shook her head. 'We wouldn't,' she said.

'You're far too useful – isn't he, Dad?'

Fraser Miles scratched his head. 'I reckon we could make a sheep farmer of him yet,' he said.

'What about me?' asked Jenny.

'Oh, you,' her father replied as he headed out into the yard. 'You're like Jess. It's in your blood.'

Jenny stopped for a moment on her way to the door. Just like Jess, she thought. Her father couldn't have paid her a bigger compliment.

Though the lambing had quietened a little, the work that afternoon was still hard, and Jess was a great help, running to and fro with his bottles of milk, feeding the lambs. There was only one interruption. A van drove up the rough track to the top field and they all turned, looking at it.

A young man with a camera got out and smiled, his eyes on Jess. 'So it's true,' he declared. 'When I heard about this I thought it was a joke.'

He introduced himself as a reporter from the local newspaper. 'Gary Baker,' he said. 'I was told that this is the puppy who featured in the recent animal welfare advertising campaign. And he's moved on to more amazing things! I'd like to take a picture of him feeding the lambs, and write an article about him, if that's OK?'

Matt laughed. 'Go ahead,' he said. 'If it's all right with you, Jen?'

Gary turned to Jenny. 'He's your dog, is he?' he asked. 'Can you tell me something about him? Does he do any more tricks?'

Jenny told the young man all about Jess.

'Wow!' he said, scribbling furiously in his notebook. 'He's had quite an exciting life for such a young pup, hasn't he? First he escaped death by a hair's breadth and now he's saving lambs! This is going to make a terrific story.'

Gary got Jenny to pose with Jess and two newborn lambs and snapped a few pictures.

'And how old are you, Jenny?' he asked. Jenny told him.

'Ah,' the reporter replied. 'So you'll be in the senior class at Graston School. You'll be going to the Graston Lass selection on Saturday, then?' he asked, conversationally.

Jenny shook her head. 'I won't be entering,'

she replied. 'I'll be too busy for that.'

Gary Baker raised his eyebrows. 'There aren't many girls of your age in Graston that would miss it,' he said cheerfully. 'You *are* an unusual girl.'

'She certainly is,' said Matt, smiling at Jenny.

Matt and Jenny waved as the reporter drove off.

'You didn't mention the Graston Lass selection to Dad and me,' Matt said, looking intently at his sister.

Jenny shrugged. 'It isn't important,' she replied. 'The lambing is much more important.'

Matt smiled at her and ruffled her hair affectionately. 'Jenny Miles,' he said. 'You're a *real* Graston lass, no matter who gets the title.'

8

It was a relief when Jake was fit enough to go back to work two weeks later. Jess had been valuable, but he didn't have Jake's experience, and never would have.

'I'm glad about that really, Jess,' Jenny murmured to the little dog as she stuck another paper flag on to a string of bunting. 'I'd much rather have you as my very own pet.' She yawned as Ellen Grace came into the kitchen.

'That's enough for tonight,' the housekeeper declared. 'You're yawning your head off, Jenny. You've been really marvellous helping me with the decorations for the common riding.'

Jenny smiled and it turned into another yawn. 'I enjoy doing the decorations,' she said. 'I'm really looking forward to the celebrations.'

'Everyone is,' said Ellen Grace. 'It means the hard work of lambing is over. Your father says things are getting much easier now. There are fewer than a hundred ewes left to lamb.'

'Ian has been great,' Jenny said. She frowned. 'Is he still out with Dad?'

Mrs Grace nodded. 'They'll be in soon,' she said. She looked thoughtful. 'I'm glad you and Ian are friends now.'

Jenny rose from the table. 'So am I,' she said. 'It's good having him around the place.'

Mrs Grace looked suddenly worried.

'What's wrong?' asked Jenny.

Mrs Grace smiled ruefully. 'It's just that I don't know if Ian and I are going to be around much longer. Calum McLay won't promise to renew my lease on the cottage and I don't know what we're going to do when it runs out.'

'You mean he's going to make you leave?' Jenny cried, shocked.

Ellen Grace shook her head. 'I don't know yet,' she confessed. 'I think that's the worst thing – the uncertainty. I've written to him to say I want an answer one way or another.'

Jenny was outraged. 'What *is* it about Mr McLay?' she demanded. 'He seems to have it in for everybody – but most of all, Dad.' Her face darkened. 'I wish I knew why.'

Ellen Grace looked at her seriously. 'You remember, Jenny, your father saying a while ago that Calum McLay has wanted to take Windy Hill from him all the while your father's lived here?' she asked.

Jenny nodded.

'Well,' Mrs Grace continued, 'Your father came to live here when he married your mother.'

Jenny looked confused. 'I don't understand,' she said. 'Why did Dad and Mum getting married matter to Calum McLay?'

Mrs Grace smiled at Jenny. 'Because Calum McLay wanted your mother to marry *him*,' she explained. 'Calum had been sweet on Sheena since he was no more than a boy. He'd even persuaded her to accept his proposal. But in the end Sheena couldn't go through with it. She left Calum at the altar and chose your dad instead, even though Fraser was very poor compared to Calum. It was a huge blow to Calum, being jilted like that.'

'I'll bet it was,' said Jenny, wide-eyed. 'Wow! So *that's* why he's got this grudge against Dad!'

'There's a bit more to it than that,' Mrs Grace went on. 'Windy Hill was your mother's family's farm. So when your mum chose to marry your dad, Calum lost a sheep farm as well as a wife. Ever since then, Calum's wanted vengeance. He went on to marry Anna – Fiona and Paul's mum, of course. But even after all these years, Calum's pride must still hurt, as it's clear he wants to take Windy Hill from your father – by fair means or foul.'

'Goodness!' said Jenny. 'I remember Dad saying that he had won a prize over Calum's head. I wonder if he meant the farm.'

Mrs Grace smiled. 'I think he probably meant your mum,' she said gently.

Jenny looked at her for a moment. 'Of course

he did,' she said. 'Oh, I wish Mum hadn't died.'

Mrs Grace put an arm round Jenny. 'Your mum was special,' she said. 'In fact, I've been meaning to tell you, I came across an old photograph the other day of your mum when she was the Graston Lass. I was one of her maids of honour that year.'

'Mum was a Graston Lass?' Jenny squeaked. 'I never knew that.'

'She certainly was,' said Mrs Grace. Jenny hovered impatiently while Mrs Grace dug in her bag and brought out a photograph and handed it to her.

Jenny looked at the old black-and-white photo and gasped. It showed a girl of about eleven, sitting on a brown pony, her long skirts draped over the pony's flank and a crown on her head. The girl was smiling, her eyes alight with laughter, and her honey-brown hair flowing down her back.

'But she looks exactly like . . .' Jenny hesitated. Maybe it was her imagination.

'She looks just like you,' Ellen Grace confirmed. 'She's the same age as you in that picture, of course. If it wasn't in black-and-white anybody would think it *was* you. You could be twins.'

Jenny felt a lump in her throat. She had seen other photographs of her mother, family photographs, but none when her mum had been eleven. 'Oh, Mrs Grace,' she began. Then she stopped, unable to go on.

'I thought you might like to keep that photo,' Mrs Grace said gently.

'Oh, I would,' said Jenny gratefully. 'I'll keep it for ever.'

Jenny heard her father and Ian come in as she went upstairs. Ellen Grace's soft voice joined in the conversation downstairs as Jenny got ready for bed. Jenny put the photograph on her bedside table and gazed at it. The resemblance really was amazing.

She turned over what Mrs Grace had told her in her mind. Now she knew what Calum McLay had against her father. Her eyes opened wide. Was that why her father had been so patient with Calum McLay that time he came to warn Fraser Miles about trespassing? Did her father feel sorry for Mr McLay? She tried to feel sorry for Calum McLay, but then she remembered that he was threatening to evict Mrs Grace, as well as battling to take Windy Hill away from them.

Jenny's eyes closed in sleep. She would think about all these problems tomorrow.

'There's a letter for you, Jenny,' Mrs Grace said the following Saturday as she laid the table for lunch.

Jenny looked up from the lamb she was feeding. There were only three lambs left in the kitchen at Windy Hill. The lambing was nearly over and it had gone better than any of them had hoped. 'A letter! For me?' she exclaimed.

She took the envelope and looked at it curiously.

'It looks official,' Ian said, impressed. 'The address is typed.'

'I wonder what it can be,' Jenny mused.

'There's only one way to find out,' Matt advised her. 'Open it.'

'Don't keep us in suspense, Jenny,' Fraser Miles smiled.

Jenny wiped her hands on her jeans and

carefully opened the envelope, drawing out a single sheet of typed paper. She scanned the letter and looked at the others in turn.

'This can't be right,' she said wonderingly. 'I didn't even enter it.'

'Enter what?' asked Ian.

'The selection,' Jenny told him. 'There must be some mistake. This letter says I'm to be the Graston Lass.'

Ian whooped with delight. 'Won't Fiona be green with envy!' he exclaimed.

'I told you that you were a *real* Graston lass,' Matt said, his face wreathed in smiles. 'Well done, Jen!'

Jenny shook her head. 'It *must* be a mistake,' she insisted.

Mrs Grace came and stood beside her. 'It isn't a mistake,' she said quietly. 'Carrie Turner wrote to the committee telling us you'd decided to help with the lambing rather than go to the selection. The committee decided Matt is right – you *are* a real Graston lass.'

Jenny looked at Mrs Grace in wonder. 'Carrie?' she said. 'And the committee didn't mind? I mean I thought you would have to be

grown-up to do a thing like that.'

'Carrie is a very determined young lady,' Mrs Grace said, smiling, 'And, besides, it was nice to have someone nominated by a person of their own age.'

'Wow!' said Jenny. 'Imagine writing to the committee! Carrie's amazing.' She looked at Ian. 'Did you know she'd done it?'

Ian grinned. 'She might just have mentioned it,' he said. 'I thought it was a great idea. It gave me something to think about too.'

'What?' asked Jenny suspiciously.

Ian just grinned even more. Jenny sighed. If he was up to something she would find out sooner or later.

Jenny looked at her father. Fraser Miles was smiling at her. 'I'm proud of you, Jenny,' he said. 'Your mother was the Graston Lass once. She would be proud of you too.'

Jenny drew in her breath. Her father *never* talked about her mother. 'Mrs Grace gave me a picture of Mum at the common riding,' she told him, shyly.

'Did she?' Fraser asked. 'I'd like to see that sometime,' he said, quietly.

'We'll frame it,' suggested Matt. 'We'll put it in a double frame with one of Jenny at *her* common riding. We'll have to get you up on Mercury soon, Jen. You know the Lass has to ride round the town and you'll need some practice. It's a long time since you've been on a horse.'

'I'll help,' offered Ian. 'The common riding is next weekend – we don't have much time.'

Jenny looked round all the eager faces. Everyone was looking at her expectantly but all she could think of was the bombshell Matt had just dropped in her lap: she would have to ride *Mercury*.

9

'I can't do it!' Jenny burst out, her mouth dry.

'Can't?' asked her father, clearly puzzled.

Jenny gazed at him. He was so proud of her, so pleased she was following in her mother's footsteps. How could she tell him she could never do it?

'I can't be the Graston Lass if it means riding Mercury,' she said at last. 'They'll have to find someone else.'

Fraser Miles leaned across and covered his daughter's hand with his own. 'I know you're nervous of Mercury,' he sympathised. 'But I thought you were beginning to like him at last. Jess likes him.'

Jenny swallowed hard. 'I don't hate him the way I used to, but nothing would make me get up on him.'

'But why not?' her father persisted.

Jenny took a deep breath. There was no way out. 'Because Mercury killed Mum,' she said in a small voice.

She saw the shock on her father's face and heard his indrawn breath but she kept her eyes steadily on him. 'You sold him because you couldn't bear the sight of him. What I don't understand is why you took him back. Mercury killed Mum and you don't seem to mind!'

Fraser Miles took a deep breath and stared down at the table for a long moment. Ellen Grace put her hand on Jenny's shoulder. Jenny was glad of the warmth of her touch. Seeing her father's shocked face was almost too much for her.

At last Fraser looked up. His eyes were

surprisingly gentle. 'Mercury didn't kill your mother,' he said softly. 'It was an accident. There was a storm, and your mother was hurrying towards Darktarn Keep. As she was preparing Mercury to jump the drystone wall below the keep, an old, dead tree nearby was struck by lightning and fell across their path. Your mum tried to turn Mercury to avoid the tree, but the horse had already got into his stride for the jump. He wasn't able to swerve in time, and had to stop dead to avoid the tree. Your mum was thrown. She hit her head on the wall and she died. It wasn't Mercury's fault. Any horse would have been terrified.'

Jenny swallowed hard. She couldn't take it in. 'How do you know all this?' she asked.

Fraser Miles spread his hands. 'I saw it, Jenny,' he said. 'I was out walking and I took shelter in the keep when the storm started. I think your mum was trying to get to the keep to do the same.'

'You saw it happen?' Jenny whispered.

Fraser Miles was silent for a long moment. 'I could see she was going to try and jump the wall. She'd done it before. Your mum was always a bit of a daredevil. I tried to call to her. I didn't think it was safe to jump in those conditions but the storm was loud. She didn't hear me. By the time I got to her she was dead.'

Jenny felt tears burn hot behind her eyes. The picture was clear in her mind – her father, running down the hill from the keep through the storm, bending over her mother's lifeless body. She couldn't bear to think of it.

'Why didn't you tell me?' she said in a low voice. 'Why did you let me think it was Mercury's fault?'

'I didn't *know* you thought that,' her father said. 'Matt and I thought you disliked Mercury because of his association with your mum's accident. We didn't know you *blamed* him. Your mother wouldn't have blamed him – and neither do I.' He rested his head in his hand for a moment. 'I'm sorry, lass. It was wrong of me not to talk to you about what happened but even thinking about it was so painful.'

'You wouldn't let me ride Mercury,' Jenny said. 'But you let Matt ride him.'

Fraser looked up at her. 'So you thought I wouldn't let you ride Mercury because he was dangerous,' he said. 'It wasn't just that, Jenny,' he confessed. 'It's true I sold Mercury right after the accident because he reminded me too much of what had happened to your mother. But the other reason I wouldn't let you ride him, even when he'd settled down, was that I knew if I saw you on Mercury it would be like seeing your mother all over again. I didn't think I could bear that.'

Tears were sliding down Jenny's face. 'But you don't mind now,' she said. 'You want me to ride him as the Graston Lass?'

Her father nodded. 'It's what your mum would have wanted,' he said. 'She would have been so proud of you, Jenny. I can't stand in the way of that. I've been wrong and I've caused you a lot of pain. I'm sorry.'

Jenny dashed the tears from her eyes. Suddenly she realised that she and her father were alone. The others must have left very quietly – probably Mrs Grace had thought of that.

'Oh, Dad,' she said. 'I wish you'd talk to me about Mum. I miss her so much.'

Fraser Miles reached over and drew Jenny

close, hugging her. 'I *will* talk about her from now on,' he promised. 'Perhaps it will help me too.'

'And I'll be the Graston Lass,' Jenny said. 'I'll do it for you – and for Mum.'

10

'There,' said Mrs Grace, setting the crown on top of Jenny's hair. 'You look really beautiful.'

Jenny blushed at the compliment as she looked at herself in the old speckled mirror at the back of Graston village hall. It was the day of the common riding and Mrs Grace had kept the promise she had made ages ago to do something with Jenny's hair.

She had brushed it till it shone and now it rippled down Jenny's back almost to her shoulder blades. Mrs Grace had caught the sides up into a loose knot that fitted under the Graston Lass crown. The crown was made of silver wire intertwined with flowers and Ellen Grace had made Jenny a long blue dress with wide sleeves and a full skirt.

'I tried to copy the one your mum wore as well as I could,' she told Jenny.

Jenny twirled in front of the mirror, the long skirt belling out round her ankles, the sleeves floating. Usually she didn't give two hoots what she wore but this was different. Today was special. 'It's lovely, Mrs Grace,' she said. 'Thank you so much.'

'Aren't you ready yet?' Ian asked, poking his head round the door of the village hall. He stopped and looked at her. 'You look like something out of an advert,' he said.

Jenny grinned. 'You look like a bandit,' she replied. She wasn't going to risk asking him what she looked like an advert for!

Ian looked down at his leather jerkin and breeches and pulled a face. 'I'm supposed to be

130

your groom,' he said. 'Come on. Mercury and Jess are waiting.'

Jenny followed him outside. As she emerged from the village hall the crowd outside cheered good-naturedly and Jenny blushed even more.

'You look great,' enthused Carrie, rushing up to her friend.

'So do you,' Jenny replied. Carrie was dressed up as a Border reiver – complete with sword.

'I'm supposed to be Jess of Beacon Brae,' Carrie grinned. 'Oops! I'd better remember to limp.'

'And, Carrie,' Jenny went on, 'thanks for nominating me. If it hadn't been for you I might never have found out what really happened to my mother. I might have gone on blaming Mercury for ever – and blaming Dad too for keeping him.'

Carrie looked serious for a moment. 'I'm glad it worked out in the end,' she said.

'Get back on your float, Carrie Turner,' yelled an official.

'Good luck!' whispered Carrie as she scuttled back to the decorated lorry and scrambled up into place.

Jenny caught her breath. The float looked great. It had a cardboard keep on it – a copy of Darktarn. Carrie was standing beside a mock bonfire with a papier-mâché torch in her hand. She waved the torch at Jenny and the other reivers around her ducked. Jenny looked closely and recognised some of her classmates. Young Paul McLay was there too, dressed as a shepherd, with a little Blackface lamb in his arms. His mother, Anna McLay, walked alongside the float. Jenny gave them all a wave.

'Playing the princess – waving to your subjects,' sneered a voice behind her.

Jenny turned. It was Fiona McLay, dressed in ordinary clothes. She had refused to take part in the pageant because she hadn't been chosen as the Graston Lass.

'Push off, Fiona,' Ian said shortly. 'Come on, Jenny. It's time to go.'

'I'm a bit nervous,' Jenny whispered to Ian as he gave her a boost into the saddle. 'Look at all these people!'

Mercury shifted slightly, then settled down. Jess was sitting patiently at the big horse's side, waiting for the fun to start.

'Don't be nervous,' said Ian. 'You look great up there on Mercury.'

Jenny smiled. At first she had still been a little nervous of the big black horse, and worried that she might have forgotten how to ride. But once she had been in the saddle for a while she had begun to feel perfectly at home – just the way she used to.

Mercury had needed to get accustomed to yet another new rider, but Ian had been a great help, and so had Jess, of course.

'Ready?' Ian asked, looking up at her.

'Ready!' she replied.

'By the way, did I tell you there might be another surprise in store for you today?' Ian asked her innocently.

Jenny looked down at him. 'What kind of surprise?' she asked.

'Wait and see,' said Ian, maddeningly. 'Walk on, Mercury!'

Jenny was so intrigued by Ian's statement she completely forgot her nervousness. She was halfway down the main street, waving and smiling to the crowds, before she realised.

Oh, well, she thought, it looks as if I'm

managing after all. But what was Ian's surprise?

Round the town and out beyond to the boundaries of Graston the procession went with crowds streaming behind. Mercury performed beautifully and Jess was in his element, trotting along beside the horse.

Jenny began to enjoy herself. The sun shone, the crowds cheered and everyone seemed to be having a great time. When they arrived back in Graston itself she was flushed with triumph and pleasure.

'Well done, lass,' her father said as Matt lifted her down off Mercury's back.

'Mercury was wonderful,' Jenny said, giving the big horse a rub.

Her father's eyes were misty. 'It's like taking a trip back in time, watching you on Mercury,' he said.

Jenny laid a hand on his arm. She knew he was thinking of her mother. 'I'm glad I did it,' she told him.

Jess scampered under Mercury's hoofs and ran round Jenny's legs. Matt laughed. 'I reckon Jess is glad too,' he said. 'I'll just go and give Mercury a rub down. I'll see you later at the sheepdog trials.'

Jenny's face lit up. Jake and Nell were both in the trials. Jake was completely recovered now and working better than ever.

'They're going to announce the Graston Hero Prize now,' Ian informed them. 'Come on, Jenny. As Graston Lass, you've got to pin the rosette on.'

Jenny looked suspiciously at Ian. His face was flushed with excitement, his green eyes sparkling.

'Why are you so interested in the hero prize?' she asked as he dragged her towards the podium in the middle of the square.

'Wait and see,' Ian replied mysteriously. 'Come on, Jess.'

Jess trotted obediently along after them. Jenny had to leave him with Ian while she took her place on the podium. The Graston Hero Prize was one of the highlights of the celebrations. It always went to someone who had done something really special.

Local vet Tom Palmer was the committee chairman. He stood up and cleared his throat, his big red face wreathed in smiles. He talked about past heroes, all of whom had done something for Graston. Then he cleared his throat again.

'This year's prize goes to a somewhat unusual hero,' he said, smiling. 'But I'm sure you'll all agree that this year's hero is very deserving. Will the Graston Hero and the person who nominated him please come up to the podium. Ladies and gentlemen, I give you the Graston Hero – Jess of Windy Hill.'

Jenny gasped in surprise as Ian led Jess up on to the podium. Almost dropping the rosette Mr Palmer handed to her, she turned to Ian.

'You nominated Jess?' she asked disbelievingly.

Ian grinned at her. 'There's nothing in the rules that says the hero can't be a dog.'

Jenny gaped at Ian as Tom Palmer read out the citation. 'For his work in saving so many lambs at Windy Hill . . . newspaper reports . . . Jess has made Graston quite famous . . . As a vet, I think it's terrific to have a doggy hero . . .'

Jenny only took in half of it. When it was time to pin on the rosette she bent down and Jess flew into her arms.

'Oh, Jess,' she murmured as she attached the ribbon to his collar. 'You're certainly *my* hero!'

'Just hold it there,' said a cheerful voice.

Jenny looked round. It was Gary Baker, the reporter from the local paper, here to cover the parade. He snapped a picture of Jenny and Jess, and grinned. 'I'm getting used to covering your dog's exploits,' he said.

Jess barked and licked Jenny's face as the crowd cheered once more.

Jenny stood back and smiled as Ian took Jess for a victory trot around the podium. She could see Matt at the front of the crowd, waving and cheering with the rest. Right at the back, a little separate from the others, were Fraser Miles and Ellen Grace. Jenny waved and they waved back.

Jenny was flooded with happiness. The lambing had been good and they wouldn't have to sell Windy Hill. Jake was fully recovered in spite of Calum McLay's dirty tricks and she and Ian were friends. She had been chosen as the Graston Lass and Jess was the Graston Hero. What a day for the Miles family!

Ian led Jess back to her and Jenny took the

puppy in her arms. Jenny saw Ian's eyes search the crowd until they found his aunt. Ian looked a little worried. Jenny remembered about the lease on Mrs Grace's cottage and frowned.

'What's wrong?' she asked.

Ian pursed his lips. 'Aunt Ellen has just told me she had a bit of bad news in the post this morning,' he replied.

'Was it a letter from Mr McLay?' Jenny asked anxiously.

Ian looked surprised. 'How did you know?' he said.

'Mrs Grace told me she was worried about her lease,' Jenny replied. 'What did the letter say?'

'Mr McLay isn't going to renew it,' Ian told her gloomily. 'Aunt Ellen is going to have to find somewhere else to live in a couple of months' time.'

'You mean she'll have to leave Graston?' Jenny asked.

Ian shrugged. 'Maybe,' he said.

Jenny turned to look once more towards the back of the crowd. She saw Ellen Grace turn and say something to Mr Miles. Her father replied, smiling down at Mrs Grace. Jenny smiled too. Maybe Mrs Grace wouldn't have to leave Graston after all. Jenny was beginning to get other ideas about that!

She bent her head to Jess and buried her face in his soft fur. 'We'll just have to see what we can do about sorting out *that* problem, won't we, Jess?' she said. 'After all, there's plenty of room at Windy Hill . . .'